Miracle's Song

Rodney LaMarr

Dedication

This book is dedicated to my lovely family. My sons who keep me on my toes. My daughter who always makes me smile and my amazing wife who stole my heart. She also pushed me to complete the book, so there's that too.

Miracle's Song

Rodney LaMarr

Book One of the California Dreaming Series

For more information on my upcoming projects, please go to my website at: www.rodneylamarr.com

Make sure you write a review wherever you purchased this book.

Table of Contents

Chapter 1

The veil of darkness blanketed the world as the eerie silence brushed over my thoughts. My chest pounded, fracturing my heart while tears skimmed my cheeks, eventually finding refuge on my lap. I peeled my hands from over my eyes, and the world slowly regained focus.

As I sat in a grey chair in the hallway of the Lancaster Police Department, the world seemed to be frozen in time. I sat staring; staring at nothing in particular. I didn't know how to feel. Was I angry, or maybe sad? Did I want revenge? Again, I didn't know what I felt, but I knew I didn't like it, whatever this was. It felt like a mysterious being was suddenly inside my chest, tugging on my heart, pulling it down, stretching it until it tore in half.

There were people in the hallway, but I couldn't hear their voices for some reason; the sound was too muffled. They were engaged in conversation about a crime or the police arresting the wrong guy or something that meant little to me. It was all just white noise that did little to drown the silence of my thoughts.

I didn't realize it, but my parents had arrived. They both embraced me but were met with little response. My dad, aware of my paralyzed state, disengaged and proceeded to speak to the officer at the front desk. As he tried to get more information, my mom held me while her tears drifted, colliding with mine. Her words were unclear; they sounded like gibberish, a mixture of unheard prayers and swears.

My dad approached again, but this time he was joined by a man dressed in a dark grey pinstriped suit. He was tall and slender, and his oversized mustache was lightly sprinkled white, reminiscent of his last pastry snack. His eyes were bloodshot as if he had been up for days. He knelt next to me.

"Hi, Miracle. I'm Detective Berry. I'd like to ask you a few questions in the back if you're up for it." He motioned to a room in the back of the hallway.

Again, I just stared. Before I knew it, my parents lifted me to my feet and we proceeded down the hall. I felt the force of gravity get stronger with every step. My father leaned in and whispered, "It'll be okay, Bubble Gum! Just breathe."

We walked into a small room with a bright fluorescent light overhead that caused me to squint. A large mirror on one wall reminded me of all the cop television shows I was accustomed to seeing. In the corner was a tripod with a camera perched on top. A red light shined from the top corner.

My parents and I sat at a table on one side and Detective Berry on the other. The detective placed a manila folder on the table. He reviewed the folder's contents for a second and sighed.

"Why did Andre aim the gun at the officers?"

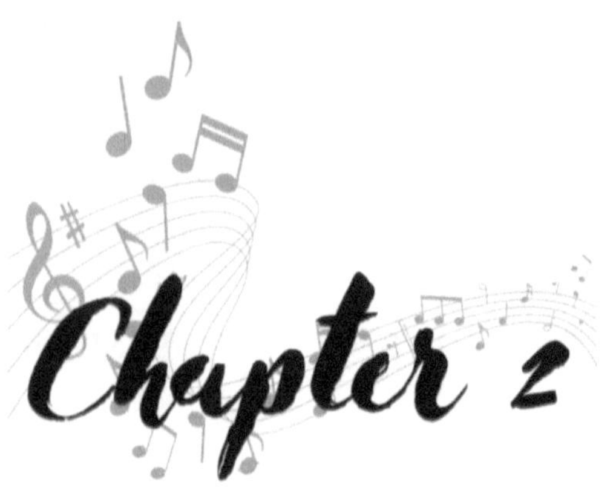

Chapter 2

The smell of ten almost-burnt pizzas filled the air as twenty high school students stood around stoves, waiting for their timers to go off. Instead of standing, I decided to take a seat at my assigned table while Greg filled me in on the craziness at his house last night.

"So, then James starts cutting Gabriel's hair with the scissors, and I'm screaming 'nooooo,' but it was too late." He hung his head down. "Mom flipped when she saw his hair." He let out a giant sigh and started shaking his head. I smiled.

"Worst big brother EVER!"

"How was I supposed to know he wanted a haircut?" We both started laughing. Our laughter was loud enough to raise the attention of our teacher, who proceeded to shush us like small children. We exchanged smiles and then he walked back to the stove to check our pizza.

"Is it supposed to be that dark?"

I shot him another smile. "You need a cooking class to prep you for this cooking class."

He scurried around clumsily, grabbing the potholders. When he opened the stove, a giant burst of black smoke blasted out, filling our area. By this time, all eyes were on us, including Ms. Lewinski. Before Greg could react, an ear-piercing buzzer rang throughout the class. The fire alarm, again. Students covered their ears, trying to avoid permanent hearing loss.

Instead of rushing all the students out the door, Ms. Lewinski ran to the phone. Her fingers quickly tapped a few numbers and she waited.

"Hey, it's me. Yeah, just a pizza. We're fine." She paused and let out a little giggle. "Yeah, him again. Thank you." She hung up the phone and gave Greg a slight smirk. The fire alarm suddenly went silent and all eyes returned to Greg.

"Take it outside, Gregory. Take it outside!" The teacher motioned towards the door and Greg rushed outside, dodging laughing students along the way. As he got to the door, he stumbled over someone's backpack, causing the pizza to fly in the air.

"This boy," I mumbled under my breath. I raised my fingers and began to count, "Three...four. Yep, four." Four times this boy has tripped today. That had to be a world record. I wondered how many times he fell when I wasn't around.

Minutes later, the classroom door swung open, and Greg reappeared. "It's fine. Everything is fine. It's still edible." Greg waved the half-burnt pizza in the air, causing small pieces of burnt crust to crumble to the floor. "See?" He ripped off a corner piece and popped it in his mouth. His eyes danced around as a giant smile spread across his face. He nodded in approval as the rest of the class just stared.

"Okay, Mr. Lowe, please take your seat," Ms. Lewinski said. When he reached our table, he shot me a big smile. "See?" he said, shoving the charred pizza in my face.

"Boy, if you don't get that charcoal out of my face…." I waved my fist in his direction. "I can't believe we're cooking partners for the entire year. There goes my A."

"Well, I'm hoping for at least a C." He peered down at the pizza. "Okay, I'd settle for a D. That's still passing, right?" Amazed by his low standards, I leaned my head against the table and closed my eyes. The familiar sound of Greg's laughter echoed in my ears and then …chewing.

Chapter 3

When the bell rang, the students poured out of the class, excited to have survived another near-emergency situation with the famous Greg and Miracle cooking duo. Greg, the ever-gracious gentleman, walked me to my locker where my bestie was waiting.

Kim leaned against my locker; her eyes glued to her geometry textbook. Her transparent glasses were barely hanging off the tip of her buttoned nose. Her brows were drawn close as her face tightened. This was her usual pose when reading something challenging.

"Does she ever *not* study?"

"Nah, that's her thing."

She peered over the book and greeted us with a warm smile as we approached. "What's up, sis?" We embraced as fake sisters would.

"Hola, lady!"

"What creations did you guys make today? Let me guess, burnt meatloaf again?"

"Nope, burnt pizza," we said in sync and we all chuckled.

"You do realize you're forming a reputation around school, right?"

"Yeah, I always thought I'd be known as the best dressed or the girl with the cutest smile."

Greg let out a little giggle that was met with my scowl. "What's so funny? You don't think I have a cute smile?" He fidgeted briefly, not knowing what to say while two girls stared him down.

"No... I meant...I love your smile...uh...like your smile."

I raised my brow. "Mmhmm."

"Was that the bell? Gotta get to class. I'll see you lovely ladies later." He scurried around the corner, disappearing in the crowd.

"Wait, I'm going to be known as the food burner now?"

"Well, technically, Greg is. You're just his partner in crime." I hung my head down in shame. Kim pressed her head against mine and squeezed. Her arm around my shoulder halted the feeling of humiliation.

After grabbing our gym clothes that were stuffed in the back of our lockers, we got dressed and strolled onto the field.

"Look, there's Autumn." Kim motioned to the bottom of the bleachers. "Taking another selfie as usual."

We walked up to meet her, trying not to interrupt the modeling session she had going on.

"Oh, snap, here they are. What it do, ladies?" She waved her phone in our direction. "Fam, y'all already know my girls, Ebony and Ivory aka White Chocolate aka Rum and Coke." I covered my face in hopes of avoiding any more public embarrassment. Kim didn't mind. She tilted her head and shot a sweet smile and a wave in the camera's direction.

Autumn returned her attention to the camera, positioning herself in various poses. The wind blew her jet-black kinky curls across her face, momentarily hiding her puckered lips. She let the camera do its magic. As she posed, her eyes widened, revealing huge pecan-brown eyes. Autumn was definitely high on the attractive scale. I fidgeted at the bottom of the bleachers, trying to smooth out the wrinkles from my clothes.

"Y'all check out my latest post on TikTok? I interviewed Jerry Cooper. Whoop whoop!" She did a little dance to show her satisfaction with herself.

Kim and I shook our heads. Of course, she interviewed the star football player. Honestly, I barely checked my TikTok, and when I did, it was mainly for all the conspiracy theories about my favorite TV shows.

Autumn would interview anyone and everyone. She had the unique ability to bring people out of their shells, no matter the situation. It was no wonder she dreamt of being the next Oprah.

"Hey, girl, I need you to ask Dre if I can interview him for a project I'm working on."

"You know you can ask him yourself, right?" I set my foot on the bottom bleachers, extending my leg to get a good stretch.

"Yeah, but you see him all the time. I don't."

"Alright, fine." I continued to stretch and made a mental note to talk to Dre at lunch.

After some push-ups and sit-ups, we were instructed to run a mile around the track. My feet caressed the ground, moving in sync with the music blaring out of my earbuds. The wind rushed over my face as my breath finally found its rhythm. The laps soon blended together. I felt weightless, like a bird soaring through the sky for the first time.

After squeezing out two miles, I searched for my friends. Kim was slumped over with her hands on her knees, panting. Her cinnamon hair covered her face as she attempted to catch her breath; she barely managed to run a mile. It was still better than Autumn who gave up after a lap and then proceeded to get back on her phone. Guess running isn't for everybody.

Chapter 4

At lunchtime, I ditched my friends to find my brother. There was only one place he would be during lunch, the basketball courts. I walked outside behind the school to the courtyard. The cool breeze brushed against my cheeks as brilliantly colored leaves danced along the ground. The sweet smell of fall reminded me of my childhood, running around with Dre as we dove in a pile of leaves dad had just raked up. I closed my eyes and took a deep breath, enjoying perfection for one brief second.

Focus, Miracle, I told myself. *Gotta find Dre.* I wished my memory a sweet farewell, hoping to relive that moment soon enough. The sound of skateboarders grinding against benches first caught my attention. Guys in baggy shorts sagging down to their butts contorted their bodies to miss colliding with other students.

Nearby, one guy protested his objections as he sprung up from the table covered in playing cards and several dice. His protest was met with resistance from a slender female wearing what looked to be a cape. She twisted her arms in a sporadic yet deliberate motion, orchestrating every moment of their game.

As I continued my journey, the sinking sensation of being watched quickly rushed over me. To my left, I saw a group of no-doubt popular girls eyeballing my outfit. After some rolled eyes and a few finger-pointing, I managed to avoid any actual contact. I was sure my New Edition t-shirt and blue jeans weren't on their to-wear list. But I didn't care.

"Yo, D up. D up."

"Watch the pick! Switch, switch," the boys shouted. Sweat poured down their faces as they focused on the guy with the ball. My eyes caught Dre as someone passed him the ball, and he lined up to shoot. Swish, three-pointer!

"Nothing but net, baby," he shouted as he high-fived his teammate. After a few more plays, the game ended with Dre's team victorious. Taking advantage of the pause in the action, I managed to wave him over.

"What up, sis?" He greeted me with our usual hand motions; a high five, a few fist bumps, backhand slaps, and a half hug.

I wrinkled my nose. "Eww, gross." Even covering my nose did little to avert the smell, my New Edition t-shirt now stained with his sweat. "What the hell?"

He laughed and tossed me his towel.

"Thanks," I said sarcastically. I wiped my t-shirt, but the towel did nothing to erase the stench. "Anyways,

Autumn wants to know if she can interview you for a project she's working on."

"Big booty Autumn?" Steam flowed from my head as I frowned in his direction. "I'm kidding…I'm kidding. Dang, so sensitive. Sure, I'll do it."

"Awesome."

"Wait, do I get paid?"

"Nope."

"Then what's in it for me?"

"You'd be helping out your sweet lil' sister, big bro." My eyes widened as my bottom lip protruded out.

"Are you constipated or something?" My fist smacked against his arm without thinking, causing him to backstep a few feet. "Dang, Mike Tyson. I'm just kidding, sheesh. This is why Mom and Dad like me more. You're too violent."

I raised my fist for another punch. This time, he raised his hands in a defensive posture. "I ain't scared of you…anymore."

"Stupid." I shook my head.

"Okay, I'll do it. I'll hook up with Autumn after school."

"Bet. Thanks, Dre." He hopped back on the court and played another game while I made my way back to my friends.

Chapter 5

My friends were hanging in our usual spot, in the east corridor of the school next to the cafeteria. It was the best place to people-watch, and I loved to people-watch.

"Hey, guys. Miss me?"

"And you are?" Kim joked.

"Har har." I squeezed between Greg and Kim on the retaining wall. Kim nudged me with her shoulder while Greg scooted over to give me more space. "So, who are we looking at today?"

Kim gestured to two guys positioned on the adjacent wall.

"Oh, Erik and his minion, Jake."

"I can't believe he's back."

This must have spiked Autumn's curiosity. She raised her head from her phone. "Back from where?"

"Suspension."

"Oh snap. What did he do?"

"Remember Rob?" Greg asked.

I scrunched my face, trying to remember a Rob. "Wait, Rob Zimmerman? Erik did that?"

Greg nodded. "Yep, almost killed the dude."

"Yeah, Rob was in the hospital for weeks. He's lucky he'll be able to walk again."

"But why? Rob's a good guy."

"Because…" Greg paused, "he was born Jewish."

Our jaws hit the floor as we let the information sink in. Our eyes suddenly all locked on to Erik while our minds circled with questions. Unfortunately, his ability to sense when he was being watched was on high alert because he began pointing in our direction.

I quickly shifted my gaze to flyers posted on a nearby bulletin board, as my other friends found their own visual distraction. All except Autumn. Her eyes remained locked on his, like a missile to its target.

It didn't take long before Erik crept towards us, with his chubby lackey slithering close behind. As the distance quickly shortened, Autumn did what she did best.

"See, Fam. Look at this piece of *you know what* in our school. Racist animals like this shouldn't be allowed here." Her camera phone was now focused on Erik.

He approached and stood mere feet away. His slim appearance was unremarkable, but the scars across his face told a thousand stories of a battered life. There were rumors about what his parents had done to him, none of them good. He cast his death-like eyes onto Autumn, causing shivers to creep over my body.

Erik listened as Autumn belittled him on camera. He merely closed his eyes and waited. When she paused, his eyes reappeared and so did the sinister smile that stretched from ear to ear. More shivers.

There was definitely something not right about this guy.

"Am I on the famous Autumn's World podcast?" he asked sarcastically, his hand now rubbing his chin stubble.

"Yeah. I want the entire world to see you in all your...." Autumn stopped to stare Erik up and down, "*glory*."

"Entire world? More like ten people at best," Erik's friend chimed in, his belly jiggling with every syllable.

"Jake is right, Autumn. No one watches your show, and personally, I don't appreciate being recorded." He reached for her phone, causing her to lose her footing and stumble backward. Greg sprang up as Jake lunged forward to cut him off.

"What are you going to do, boy?" Jake's jaw clenched as veins pulsated in his neck. Without thinking, my hands found their way to Erik's chest, pushing him back out of range of Autumn.

Erik stumbled but quickly readjusted. His eyes met mine, and he lurched out towards me. My hands shaded my face from any blows, but the punches never came. I looked up to see Jake holding Erik at bay.

Erik looked at Jake's hand on his chest in disgust. He relaxed his shoulders when Jake nodded towards two teachers passing by. The redness in Erik's usually pale face subsided.

"Guess we'll have to finish this another time." Then, Erik turned his attention back to me. "But if you ever touch me again, I will kill you." His eyes narrowed, and a grim smile crossed his face. "I will kill you, little girl!"

My knees weakened, and the ground felt unsettled. Erik's icy stare made my hands tremble, and the best they could do was find refuge behind my back. Suddenly my body was jerked back as firm hands pressed against my waist. I turned to see Greg pulling me as he moved to shield me from this monster.

Greg's towering frame forced Erik to tilt his head up to meet Greg's eyes, but he didn't cower. His jaw tightened and his eyes narrowed. Erik began to study him as a predator studies its prey. But he didn't need Greg to react. He knew he had scared him and that was what Erik thrived on...fear.

Neither of them moved or spoke a word. The tension rose like the new day's sun.

Suddenly, a loud ringing interrupted the heavy silence. It was the school bell and lunch was over. Erik still didn't budge. He just stood there, staring into Greg's soul, looking for something to latch on to.

I placed my trembling hand on Greg's shoulder, which shook like a California earthquake but he hid it well. I leaned in. "Let's go, Greg." I picked up his backpack and held it out in front of him. "Greg." My voice was soft yet stern and it worked. He grabbed his bag and slowly walked away, leaving Erik and his friend still staring, still smiling.

Chapter 6

Moments later, I sat in History class as Mr. Williams stood in the front of the classroom, scanning his students. "So, Reverend Bevel did most of the coordination, which was quite impressive if you think about it." He turned to face the smart board once again and continued the video.

My mind, unable to concentrate, replayed our close encounter with Erik and his goon. I wondered, "How can people like him still exist? How could someone hate so much that it swallows them whole?"

Don't get me wrong, I knew there was racism everywhere, even in Lancaster. But it just surprised me how blatant it was. I remembered visiting my grandma in Arkansas and seeing the Klan walking down the street carrying a giant cross like it was no big deal. One might have thought the South would be much worse, but that was the South; of course, there would be racism there.

Despite my best efforts, I knew I couldn't solve the nation's racism problem that day, so eventually, my mind came back down to Earth. I was able to focus my attention on my schoolwork.

Once class ended, I found Greg walking down the hall. I caught up with him and grabbed his arm to get his attention. He lurched forward and whipped his head around.

"Why are you so jumpy?" He gave me a worried glance while searching for the correct answer. Realizing he was still shaken up from before, I dropped the subject. "Anyways, thanks for earlier. You didn't have to do that." His eyes relaxed and he smiled his sweet smile.

"It's all good. It was nothing."

"Well, thanks anyway. Alright, gotta go. Ms. Slack hates for people to be late. See ya."

"Yeah…see ya."

As I fought the tide of students racing to their class, I waved to a friend heading to her class, and then something caught my eye. It was Greg. He was still in the same spot as if his feet were frozen. His body jerked from left to right as fellow students bumped into him while trying to move around his still body. When my eyes reached him, he quickly averted his eyes and turned to walk away.

"That's weird," I thought.

Later that day, I met Kim in front of the school bus and we made our way to our usual seats in the back. Since we were the first picked up in the mornings, we were also the last two stops in the afternoon. Greg sat in front of us, talking to one of his friends about the latest zombie movie.

Kim pulled out her English book, trying to get a head start on her homework, while I pushed my earbuds in and pressed shuffle on my phone. I closed my eyes and rested my head against the seat in front of me. The coolness of the leather felt refreshing against my forehead.

Soon, the sound of the students on the bus was drowned out by the soulful voice of my favorite singer, Willow Marie. Her soft voice caressed the beat as the song played, making a beautiful combination.

As the bus departed, my body jerked forward and then back. My shoulders dropped, and all the day's stress slowly disappeared into the music. Music was always the key to my soul's treasure chest. It freed my mind and caused whatever hardships I faced to vanish. And for that brief moment, I was free.

As the music continued, a strange cold sensation tingled throughout my body and the darkness grew darker. Suddenly, my soul plunged deep inside my inner being as my mind went blank. The music vanished. All that remained was a deathly silence.

Chapter 7

The faint sound of singing slowly crept back into existence; but Willow Marie was no more. Instead, there was only one angelic voice, that of a little girl.

Her voice was soft and flowed to the rhythm of my heartbeat. As the singing intensified, so did the number of children, their voices seeping joy and happiness.

Heat pressed against my face, as if the sun had gently kissed my cheek. My eyes slowly unglued as the brightness of the day became a stark reality. All I could do was use my hand as a shield to ease the sun's effects, but it still took a few minutes to fully adjust.

The bus was no more; instead, my feet were firmly planted on the ground. My heart pounded through my chest while I tip-toed on the verge of hyperventilating. My mind zipped from one thought to another, not truly knowing if this was reality or not.

Was I kidnapped? Was I drugged?

My mind raced with questions.

Wait…was it aliens? Dang, was Greg right this whole time? I shook my head in disbelief. There's no way Greg could be right.

Breathe, girl! I thought. *Breathe!*

I closed my eyes and focused on my breathing (an old trick learned from running) deep and deliberate breaths. Inhale. Exhale. Inhale. Exhale. My heartbeat gradually returned to normal as my thoughts became more apparent.

I let out one final big breath and scanned my surroundings. Modest brown brick buildings nestled between white-walled stores stood on the opposite side of the street. I was met with giant trees dancing with the wind as birds sang their own sweet melody. The refreshing aroma of pine filled the air, which reminded me of being at grandma's house on a hot summer day.

I move along the sidewalk to observe the cars along the street. My dad would have loved these.

"Classics," I mumbled.

Classics that were in pristine shape, as if they were brand new. The shimmer of the sun reflected off a white-painted car captured my attention.

"Buick Riviera."

Moving to the back of the car, I noticed its license plate.

Alabama. That's strange. I checked out the rest of the cars to realize they all showed the same thing, Alabama.

Okay, we figured out where we are. Go brain! I gave myself a silent cheer, one piece of the puzzle solved.

I closed my eyes again to concentrate.

"What else, Miracle? Think!" Then suddenly, it hit me. The singing. It was close, like around the corner close. I could still hear the children off in the distance.

"Here goes nothing."

I raced towards the music, still looking at my surroundings and figuring out where I was. I eyed the street sign: 16th Street North.

As I turned the corner, the singing grew thunderous. I peered down the street and my jaw dropped. There the children were, hundreds, if not thousands of kids piling out of what appeared to be a school.

Kids as young as six to teenagers filled the street, merging into one giant unit. The rush of their energy hit me like a brick wall. Excitement filled the air as they began marching down the street, their faces filled with smiles and laughter.

Some were dressed in ordinary clothes, while others sported freshly ironed clothes and nicely combed hair as if it was picture day. I stood there still in awe of what I was witnessing. If the sheer number of kids didn't surprise someone, their singing would have. The reverberation magnetized their voices against nearby buildings.

"Ain't gonna let no jailhouse turn me 'round,
Turn me 'round, turn me 'round.
Ain't gonna let no jailhouse,
turn me 'round."

There was excitement in their voices, a type of happiness and joy that is rare nowadays. They continued.

"I'm gonna keep on a-walkin',
keep on a-talkin,'
Marchin' on to freedom land!"

I gawked at the parade of children as a young girl nearly knocked me over trying to catch up to her friends. She stopped momentarily and turned her attention to her untied shoe. As she knelt down, her pigtails dangled, covering her maple brown cheeks. Her head shot up and she shouted, "Hey, guys. Wait for me."

This was my chance.

"Excuse me, what's going on?" I reached out my hand and tapped her on her shoulder. She slowly stood up and turned to face me. That was when I saw her eyes. The most amazing light brown eyes I had ever seen. They were truly unforgettable. As she greeted me with a smile, she faded into darkness. Her world vanished, as did the singing. Again, the soul-sinking feeling hit me like a freight train and the darkness returned.

Seconds later, my once steady stance was replaced with the familiar jerking motion of the school bus. The sound of nearby students and the familiar afternoon traffic slowly faded into existence. I snapped my head back, looking for the little brown-eyed girl, but she was gone.

"Girl, you okay?" Kim took her head out of her book and focused her deep-set blue eyes on me, puzzled.

"Yeah, I...I just had the weirdest dream." I knew deep down it was no dream, but nothing else made sense. Nothing else could explain how real it was. I pressed my hand against my cheek and could still feel the warmth of the sun. "Yeah, just a dream."

Chapter 8

After school, I stepped inside our three-bedroom apartment to find my parents sharing a few kisses in the kitchen.

"Oh, gross! Can't y'all do that somewhere else?" I said, scrunching up my face. I threw my keys on the end table and proceeded to the dining room.

"Sure can," my dad said, giving my mom a wink. She looked up, cheeks flushed, and got lost in his eyes. He wrapped his arms around her as she began rubbing his back. After 24 years of marriage, these two still acted like young high schoolers, falling in love for the first time, every time.

Moments later, my father finally looked up from their embrace and looked at his precious daughter recoiling at the table. I shook my head and wrinkled my nose once again.

"How was school, Bubble Gum? Wait…where's your brother?"

"School was school." I pulled a grape from the fruit filled wicker basket in the middle of the table. "Dre's helping a friend with a project, so he'll be late."

"He could have let us know. I'm making meatloaf," my mom said, still leaning on my dad's chest.

"Well, I'll have his piece then. No one skips out on my baby's meatloaf." He gave her a little squeeze.

"I know that's right. My meatloaf is good, huh?" She tilted her head as she shot me a wink. She then unglued herself from my dad's chest and reached into the cabinet, pulling out pots and pans. My dad just leaned against the counter, staring at his lovely bride.

My mom was a fantastic cook. I would have her teach me, but she brought up her childhood and all of our family history every time I joined her in the kitchen. It was cool to a point, but I got tired of hearing about our great aunt or my cousin twice removed. I was more of a future type of girl.

"How was work, guys," I asked while pulling out my backpack and sprawling my books on top of the table.

"Girl, you know we are about to eat. Get your stuff off the table."

"Mom, meatloaf takes like five hours to cook. I'll be done with my homework and most of high school before dinner's even ready." My dad grinned as my mom crossed her arms and frowned. "I mean, yes ma'am," I said, shoving my stuff back in my bag.

"Work was good on my end. The front office bought Larry a cake for his birthday. But don't worry, babes.

I didn't ruin my appetite. I only had two pieces." My mom stared at my dad's belly and frowned. He wasn't fat. He was somewhat muscular, like he used to work out a lot but skipped a few days here and there. "Babes, it was his birthday! I can't be the only one not honoring Jeremy."

"You said Larry," I interrupted.

"Larry. Jeremy. Whatever his name is, we had cake!" We all laughed at his notoriously lousy sense of humor.

"Mom, anything exciting happen today. Like a bank robbery?"

"Girl, do you want there to be a bank robbery? I'm jumping out the window if anyone comes into the bank with a weapon. Gun, bomb, heck even if they look like they have a cold, I'm out."

I giggled at the thought of this 5-foot 3 woman jumping out a window.

"Work was fine," she continued. "But I can't wait for the weekend to get here."

"Are we doing anything?"

"Nope. I just don't want to go to work anymore."

"Yeah, I can't wait to retire," my dad said.

"When are y'all retiring?" I asked. I flung another grape in my mouth.

"Depends. When are you and Dre moving out?" My dad shot a smile at my mom as she just stared in his coffee brown eyes. "What? These kids are expensive." His laughter continued.

My mom rolled her eyes and went back to prepping dinner, but my dad grabbed her once again and stole a kiss.

"Gross!" I gathered my school supplies and stormed out of the room. As I got to the corner, I paused and looked back. There they were. Two young loves embracing each other as if the rest of the world didn't exist. Their love was an eternal type of love. It was romantic, and I hoped that I'd find it too one day.

Chapter 9

The door slid open as the chime announced our presence. We flashed the clerk a quick smile as we bypassed the other customers. A few more steps, and there we were, the nacho bar.

"Red?" Dre asked while reaching for a gigantic plastic cup. He didn't even bother to wait for a response. He already knew. As the icy goodness poured from the spout, I grabbed a container of three-day-old tortilla chips and proceeded to cover them with flaming hot melted cheese.

"The food of the Gods." Dre stared as the cheese erupted over the chips.

We quickly paid for our items and headed on our way.

We were halfway to Kim's when it hit. "Awwhhh." The intense pain consumed my brain like a zombie on the brink of an apocalypse. My eyes flung shut as I pressed my palm against my left eye. "Too fast! Too fast," I shrieked.

Dre grabbed the cup from my hand, staring at me as he slurped away.

"Amateur. You gotta drink it slowly."

"The pain." I let out a weird laugh-cry.

"We get Slurpee's almost every weekend. How do you not know this by now?" He tossed a few chips in his mouth, tilting his head to avoid the cheese from dripping to the ground.

As my mind defrosted, I reached for another sip to find an empty plastic cup in my brother's hands. "What the…"

Dre shot an inquisitive look in my direction and then grabbed the cup again. He placed his lips over the straw and the annoying sound of slurping drowned my frustration.

"Awh. Yeah, you need to learn to share, sis." He tossed the cup in a nearby trashcan and kept on strolling.

I shook my head. "Well, at least hand me a…" Before I could finish, the nacho container plunged into the trash too.

I really have to buy my own food from now on, I reminded myself.

After a few choice words, we continued our trip. There wasn't much to look at along Sierra Highway. An old furniture store sat on our right, while the sidewalk across the street was lined with Fremont Cottonwood trees and small bushes. Beyond the trees was a vast dirt field with a few Joshua trees scattered here and there. The joys of living in the Mojave Desert, I guess.

Dre paused and peered off in the distance. He slid his foot atop the abandoned railroad tracks as his eyes ran parallel with the steel lines. Dre was always amazed by those tracks. They were a sign of freedom and adventure for him, something he felt he lacked in beautiful Lancaster, California. His mind was lost in another journey, a journey of what-ifs.

"One day," he paused. "I'm going to see the world: Paris and New Zealand. Oh, Africa, can't forget Africa." His head nodded in agreement with his own thoughts.

I stood next to him, shoulder to shoulder. "Can't forget Africa." I leaned against him as his mind wandered.

When we reached Kim's apartment, she was already waiting for us by the community pool. Her long frizzy hair barely hid her head, buried in another book. Her hair danced to the beat of her reading as if the book was somehow speaking to her. Her eyes flashed from one side to another as her brain undoubtedly consumed every word.

"Does she ever *not* study?" Dre asked.

"Nah, that's her thing."

Without missing a beat, her eyes peeked over the pages, and she greeted us with her usual sweet smile. The reflection of her braces caused a sparkling effect, enhancing her smile. I wrapped my arms around her and she returned the greeting.

"Aight, I'm going to find Rieko." Dre shot us a wave and headed around the corner.

"What's up, chica? What are you studying now?"

"Oh, this is for fun." She flashed the cover in front of me: *First Things First.*

"Hmmm, never heard of it."

"It's about lawyer stuff."

"Oh yeah. My Kimmie, the lawyer."

Her cheeks turned red as she let out a little giggle, "Whatever."

"You are going to be a great lawyer. Your head is always in the books. And you're, like, the most honest person I know." Her head perked up. "Plus, when I'm rich and famous, I'll need a good lawyer because I plan on doing a lot of stupid stuff." I extended my hand, and she pressed hers against mine. Our friendship was fueled by laughter and loyalty. Kim wasn't my best friend...she was family.

Chapter 10

Moments later, we heard strange shouting coming from around the corner. Among the raised voices, one was too familiar.

Dre.

We quickly grabbed our stuff and raced around the corner.

As we approached, our eyes found Dre standing nose to nose with another familiar face. Erik! I forgot he lived in the same neighborhood. And of course, Jake was standing next to him, but this time, he had a snarling monster of a dog accompanying him.

Our arrival did little to disturb the tense situation, but Jake noticed Kim instantly. His finger shot in her face as he taunted, "Looks like you're playing for the wrong team, missy."

"Maybe she just likes dark meat." Erik's monotone voice caused every word to be that much creepier.

Kim folded her arms, not impressed by their ignorant remarks.

Jake's dog flashed its predatory teeth and lunged forward, sending drool flying everywhere. Caught off guard, Kim's eyes widened as she jumped back and blood rushed from her face. It was mere inches away from her when Jake jerked the metal chain that restrained the wild creature, possibly saving her from a disastrous situation.

Dre pivoted to see if Kim was okay. Her eyes were locked on the dog and for good reason too. Dre turned back to Erik. His eyes flashed with fire, nostrils flared, and his hands curled into balls. "If you want to go, let's go then!"

Dre adjusted his body to create a smaller target for his opponent. He lowered his chin as he swayed side to side, bouncing on the balls of his feet.

Jake tensed up, clenching his jaw. His body now matched Dre's. But Erik didn't budge, he wasn't afraid of the taller adversary. Erik lowered his head but kept his eyes on Dre. Then, he slowly crept forward. Dre moved back, eyebrows raised.

As Erik slithered forward, heavy footsteps pounded against the pavement, etching closer and closer. A broad-shouldered giant of a man came into view, wielding something in his hand.

Rieko took his place alongside my brother, catching his breath from his short sprint. He stretched out his muscular arm, revealing his new weapon of choice. The sun's reflection hit the machete perfectly, shining a harsh light in Erik's face. Erik paused his forward movement and peered down at the weapon. Unimpressed, his eyes jerked back to Dre, and there it was. His devilish smile shook my core as my heart trembled with fear.

Erik dropped his grin and stood void of any emotion. His body remained relaxed as his eyes shot daggers at my brother. Time seemed to freeze; seconds seemed like minutes; minutes seemed like hours. The four boys stood frozen to the pavement, waiting for any sign of increased aggression. Finally, Erik turned and gave Jake a nod and then they turned back to face Dre.

"We'll see each other real soon, my friend."

Dre nodded, turning the right corner of his mouth up. Meanwhile, Jake faked a smile in Rieko's direction as he pulled his still-growling dog back. Kim's eyes flashed from Erik to Jake to the dog. I guess she didn't know who the more significant threat was.

As Erik turned his body to walk away, he paused as if he suddenly realized I was there. His eyes locked on mine as I shrunk into a miniaturized version of myself, trying to escape his field of vision.

"Hey, little girl." He pointed a finger in my direction and screwed his face.

"Don't talk to her! Don't you ever talk to my sister, ya hear me?"

"You're sister, huh? Interesting." Dre lunged forward, but Rieko's gigantic hand restrained him.

Erik smiled another evil smile and then slowly walked away, his shadow following close behind.

Dre twisted his body, shaking out of Rieko's grip, and paced back and forth, exhaling deeply. Rieko turned to Kim and me to make sure we were okay. Kim's hand covered her mouth in disbelief as her mind began to wander. I noticed her hands were shaking as they pressed against her lips.

Rieko looked me over and then turned back to Dre.

"Hey, Rieko?"

"Yeah? You alright, Miracle?"

"Where the hell did you get a machete?"

Dre halted, looking down at Rieko's hand. Then Kim did the same. Rieko looked down and then skimmed our puzzled faces. Finally, we allowed ourselves to share one very much needed laugh.

Chapter 11

After our close encounter, Kim and I went back to her apartment as Dre and Rieko stayed at the pool. When we walked in, we greeted her dad and proceeded straight to her room. She began watching TV, but I grabbed my earbuds from my bag and sprawled across her twin-size bed. My heart still raced from the encounter with Erik, so I chose to turn to my usual escape— music.

The bass of the music rattled my bones as my heart gradually returned to normal. I faintly heard the TV in the background. But as I turned up the volume, the beat overpowered all other sounds in existence.

The bass pounded against my eardrums as the rapper's fast-paced flow caused my body to sway without thought. My eyes slowly closed, shutting out the darkness of the world. And then…

The falling feeling rushed over me as my soul sank within itself. Cold shivers ran across my body as a familiar feeling reappeared.

My eyes slowly opened, revealing a new world. The sun glared high in the sky, projecting an intense heat, which blanketed over everything, including me. Sweat dripped from my forehead, causing a burning sensation in my eyes. It was definitely summer.

Stretched out before me stood a vast field, sprinkled with white as far as the eye could see. I took a deep breath in and a unique smell danced in the air. It wasn't sweet or fresh, just unique. My fingers ran against the smooth skin of the vegetation leaves.

"Cotton?"

Then, I saw them. Men, women, and even children spread along the field in perfectly uniformed rows. Sweat glistened off their faces onto their already drenched clothing.

They crouched down, pulling the little white material off the vegetation and placing them into large brown sacks. I knew then where I was. I was amongst slaves; my ancestors. I stood there speechless, not knowing what to do, my shock interrupted by their voices.

"Wade in the Water...
God's a gonna trouble the water.
See dat band all dressed in white
God's gonna trouble the water."

Their voices were not of pain and hopelessness; quite the opposite. There was strength in their voices. I was taken aback by this. If this was indeed slavery, then why sing of joy? Joy didn't exist; at least not here, not now.

Suddenly, a loud whistle blew through the air, interrupting all work. The group wiped the pouring sweat that puddled at their feet and proceeded to gather up their belongings. The wave of people walked to tattered-down wooden sheds, which I assumed were their homes. I joined.

Out of the corner of my eye, I noticed a group of black men and women huddled around each other. Clapping and laughter were heard, but it wasn't coming from them. In front of them stood a white elderly man with a long white beard dressed in a button-down shirt with an opened black vest. He was whooping and hollering as two young men joined along. On the side of him was a young blonde girl. She couldn't have been more than six or seven years old.

"Why they dancing, pa?" She had a rich southern accent.

He dropped down to one knee, steadied by his wooden cane. His arm slung over her as he leaned her close to him. "Eliza, they dancing for a piece of cake." He gestured towards the young man dancing back and forth, gyrating his body for the audience's approval. "Ya see, the one who can dance the best will get a piece of dis here cake."

"But they dancing funny, pa," she scrunched her face, unimpressed.

"I know, suga'. They can't dance." A crusty laugh escaped his lips. "They trying to dance like us but they too dumb, baby girl." The older man kissed her cheek softly and continued clapping.

Outrage poured over me. Being a slave was terrible enough...now they had to dance for food? I balled up my fists and stepped forward. My movement was brought to a halt by a weathered hand filled with wrinkles and scars clutching against mine. It felt rough, as if it had seen nothing but hard labor all its life. I followed the hand up to see an older woman locking her eyes on mine. Her face was a twin to her hands.

"Hush up, darlin'. Don't be causing no trouble round hur."

"But what he's doing isn't…." I began to speak, but she gave me the same look my grandma gives when I'm about to say something stupid. I knew not to finish that statement.

The old woman didn't respond. Her eyes set upon mine as she brought her finger to her lips and whispered, "Hush up now!" I nodded.

I felt as if my grandma had just scolded me. I held my head down. The old woman stood still, holding my hand. Her tattered white dress engulfed in dirt hung loosely on her malnourished frame. Her hair was also filled with dirt, and she had visible cuts and bruises on her arms. She leaned towards me and whispered, "We be doing the cake dance." A cheek-filled smile crossed her face, revealing several missing teeth.

"Yeah, but why are they laughing?" I asked.

"Because massa' thinks we too stupid to know how to dance, but we's be making fun of how they dance." Her shoulders bounced almost uncontrollably with every laugh.

I concentrated on the dancer once again. Then, I turned to the other slaves in the background. Smiles adorned their faces as they enjoyed the secret held amongst themselves.

"See?" The lady flashed me a gum-filled smile.

As the old white man continued clapping, two black men danced in front of each other playfully. Each man topped the next, move for move. The old man continued to cheer with glee while the old lady smiled with guilty pleasure.

Unimpressed by the chaotic scene, the little girl shook her head and turned her attention to three little black girls who played off in the distance. She smiled in their direction, with the gleam of pure innocence that lives in the heart of children. As I turned back to the dancers, darkness fell once more as my soul sunk into a non-existent world.

Chapter 12

The following weekend, Dre and I headed back to Kim's apartment. She was supposed to help me study for Monday's Geometry test while Dre hung out with Rieko. But first, we had to quench our thirst with some red Slurpee magic.

As we entered the convenience store, the little bell at the top of the front door announced our arrival. We shot the cashier a smile and made our way to the back. Before we could make it all the way, I stopped in my tracks, causing Dre to slam into me.

"What are you doing?"

I gestured to the back of the store. His eyes traced my field of vision and he saw our favorite two people; Jake and Erik.

"Let's get out of here."

"Nah, they aren't going to force us out. We good. Red, right?" I looked up at Dre, but didn't respond. "Red, right?" he repeated. I nodded, still not comfortable with the situation.

Dre continued to the nacho bar, eyeing his rival from a distance, making sure he could see him at all times. The skinheads grabbed their items and headed to the front of the store. Erik shot Dre a cold stare but paid him no mind.

"Yeah, and give me a package of Ultras," he ordered the clerk behind the counter, a young Indian man wearing a Los Angeles Lakers jersey. The man hesitated but kindly obliged.

Jake ripped the corner of his wrapper and slid the end of a licorice stick between his lips. His black shirt slid up slightly, revealing his frumpy body, reminding me of Slimer from those old Ghostbuster movies. He scrunched up his face in our direction and began chuckling.

After the transaction was complete, they quickly grabbed their stuff and left without incident. My shoulders relaxed. I sighed. As soon as the two were out of sight, I turned to Dre.

Whack!

"Ouch, what's that for?"

"That's for acting tough, lil' boy. You're outnumbered, Dre!"

"What? Two of them," he motioned between us, "and two of us."

"Me?" I pointed to myself, surprised. "Boy, you know I'm a lover, not a fighter."

His face grew stern as he shot me a death stare.

"What? Oh, not like that." His face relaxed as he proceeded to grab the nachos.

Moments later, we continued down the path. Suddenly, a black jeep quickly passed, kicking up dirt in our direction. A blanket of dust and sand covered the air, forcing us to turn our heads. Our hands covered our faces as we shut our eyes.

Unexpectedly, Dre jumped back. A flying object made its way past my elevated hand and found the perfect resting spot on my cheek. I jolted backward. Steaming hot beans and cheese slid down my face as Dre looked on in disgust.

"Oh snap," Dre said.

"What the hell!"

The jeep slid to a halt momentarily as someone flashed a stubby middle finger in the passenger side window. Then, the jeep slowly moved forward, as Dre's eyes scanned my targeted face and the jeep. Without thinking, he reached down and grabbed a rock. His aim was perfect, shattering the passenger side mirror. Glass fell to the ground as the jeep slammed on the brakes. Then, it reversed rapidly. We could see the driver's eyes in the side mirror. They were honed on Dre and filled with anger.

We hurled our bodies onto the dirt path as the jeep approached, avoiding a near collision. The smell of gas filled the air as the jeep screeched to a halt. The doors flung open and Erik and Jake jumped out.

"Oh, you're in for it now, boy," yelled Jake as he pointed a bat in our direction.

They approached us with slow, deliberate steps. A smile stretched from one ear to the other as Erik pointed a metal crowbar at us. I reached for Dre's arms, but he shrugged me off.

"Dre!" His jaw tightened. His face was unrecognizable. There was something in him I had never seen before. His eyes froze on the two aggressors and he mumbled something.

"What?" No response. "Dre, what did you say?!?!"

His eyes still locked on the two, he said, "I fear for my life."

My eyes went between him and the two. "What?" Erik was roughly ten yards away. Terror mounted with every step.

"I fear for my life and yours. Do you hear me?"

My heart pounded through my chest. Dre lost it. He stood there motionless. I screamed again, "Dre!" I tried to fight the rising panic as my body shivered. I drew in a shaky breath and prepared myself for a fight.

Then…the world stopped. Birds paused mid-flight, freezing in time. Clouds hung in the sky like paintings in a museum. Erik's left foot floated inches away from the ground as Jake's body momentarily paused with his arm stretching out.

And then…a powerful noise burst into existence, bouncing against my eardrums, vibrating my inner being. The noise lingered in the air, finding its home in the depths of my existence. I didn't turn my head. There was no need.

This sound…this unmistakable sound could only come from one thing.

Chapter 13

The faces of the two approaching teens turned ghost white. Their eyes bulged as fear spread across their faces. Erik skid in the dirt, unable to come to a complete stop. Small pebbles kicked up underneath his feet. His legs gave way, and he fell to the ground while his eyes stayed forward. Before fully recovering, he pressed himself up and ran to the jeep, disappearing into the vehicle.

As the jeep quickly vanished from view, Jake remained motionless, his eyes locked on Dre's. He peered down to his hands, patting his chest, looking for the entry wound. His mouth was wide open as tears ran down his face.

"Oh my God!" he screamed out. "Oh my God!" Jake's breathing changed. His chest heaved up and down.

My eyes examined Jake's body, searching for the crimson pool. Jake staggered and eventually dropped to one knee…and then the other. "Oh my God," he repeated. Still in shock, Jake took one final look in our direction. His eyes rolled back as he fell to the ground. His face bounced off the dirt, and then he was motionless.

My heart pounded uncontrollably, like a thoroughbred that could not be tamed. My breath became frantic as I peered over to my brother. The smoke was still ascending from the gun as his arm remained stiff, still aimed at where the skinhead used to be standing.

"DRE," I screamed, "what did you do?"

He stood there motionless, unable to grasp the horrific act he just performed. My hero had taken a life. To protect me. He had killed him.

"DRE," I repeated.

Dre lowered his arm and looked at me.

"RUN!"

The city zoomed past us as we flew over the neighborhood, passing stores, streetlights, and even the train tracks. The usual twenty-minute walk seemed like it took just brief moments. It wasn't until my feet touched the bottom of Kim's steps that the world became clear again. My body slumped over the metal rail as Dre sat on the bottom step. His head hung between his knees while he tried to catch his breath.

"Dre." I took a breath, but my breathing wasn't fully recovered yet. "What were you…? What were you doing?"

His only reply was, "I don't know. I don't know." He looked into my eyes without saying another word. His eyes were cloudy, filled with confusion and uncertainty. For the first time, I saw fear in his eyes. I placed my hand on his shaking shoulder.

"I won't tell anyone." He nodded and continued panting.

"Come on, let's get inside." I reached for his hand to help him up. He pulled me into him, wrapping his arms around me as he stood.

"It wasn't supposed to go down like that." I could feel his body trembling like a scared little boy.

We made our way halfway up the steps when we were interrupted by a recognizable chirping sound that sent shivers down my spine.

Chapter 14

I turned to see a matte black Chevy Tahoe with blue and red lights flashing and "POLICE" written in giant lettering along the side.

"Hey, you! Stop right there," the words echoed out. The voice was stern and authoritative.

Dre took a deep breath and descended down the stairs, taking slow and deliberate movements. Two officers, still in their police vehicle, were eyeing us up and down. One officer, a mid-thirties white male with a buzzcut and thick mustache that stretched over his lip, got out of the car. The sun glistened off his badge, which was hugged by a black band with a blue line set in the middle. He adjusted his waist belt and mumbled something into the walkie-talkie slung over his shoulder.

"Can we help you, Officer?" I forced myself to stay calm…act calm…act innocent.

"Where are you two coming from?" the driver asked while getting out of the vehicle.

"Coming from our house. Down Avenue K, sir." I shot Dre a glance, but he just stood there like a statue, only his bottom lip shivered. I turned back to the cops and smiled.

"Avenue K, huh?" By this time, both officers were out of their car and positioned themselves apart, one slightly angled in front of us and the other slightly to the side of us. The second officer, a middle-aged male with deep-set eyes, scowled. His eyes constantly scanned right then left, as he let his partner do the talking.

"What are you doing in this area?"

"We have friends in the neighborhood. I'm going to their house to study." His eyes were locked on mine. His face showed no emotion, but they shared glances between the two. "Know anything about Geometry?" I said with another smile.

"Mmhmm. Uh, where are your books?" The driver began to stare at Dre.

"Oh, I'm just going to use my friend's. She's supposed to quiz me, so no need for two books." I shot both officers a smile.

Please believe this, I thought to myself.

"I've never seen a girl like yourself study Geometry," Buzzcut said. His accent was distinct but hard to place; maybe Texas. His partner grimaced at the comment. I knew what "girl such as yourself" meant, but this wasn't the time to be all Malcolm X. Nope, not right now.

"What's wrong with you, boy?" All eyes turned to Dre. I tried to shoot telepathic notes to him to speak, but it didn't work. Buzzcut began stepping forward as I saw the other slowly lower his right hand to his waistband.

"Boy?"

"His name is Dre. Right Dre?" I gently nudged him, hoping to bring this statued-soul back to life.

"Andre," he mumbled, still staring off in the distance.

"What did you say?"

"My name. Andre." Dre looked down at me. "Sir."

I nodded in appreciation and took another breath.

"Well, Andre, what are you doing here? You don't look like the biology type."

"Geometry, sir," Dre corrected him. I'm glad his mind was back to full power, especially since he was unfazed by the officer's childish attempt to trick us. "But I do study Biology as well." He smiled. "Sir."

The officer's hands returned to a neutral position and Buzzcut ceased his approach.

"Mmhmm. Well, you kids get out of here."

"And stay out of trouble."

"Always, sir." He nodded. I turned to Dre and motioned up the stairs.

There were exactly twelve steps to Kim's door. Twelve steps. That was it. While Dre proceeded to step eleven, the back of his shirt flapped open. And there it was…

"Gun!"

Chapter 15

The shout was deafening. I turned to see both officers reach for their waistbands. Then I turned to Dre. He jerked forward, waving his empty hands in front of him. His fingers stretched out, revealing no weapon. His face said it all; he was terrified.

"No, no, it's not what it looks like," he pleaded.

The officers started talking over each other but commanding the same thing; for Dre to drop the gun and get on the ground.

Dre's arms flung towards the sky, and he closed his eyes. His face tensed up. He waited for the shots, but no bullets came, just more commands.

"Lower the weapon slowly!"

"Get down, now! Do you hear me? Now!"

"Lower it, boy!"

Dre screamed, "Okay, I'm listening. I'm obeying. Okay, calm down, please."

Tears poured down my face as the butterflies in my stomach did summersaults. My chest was heavy, and I couldn't breathe.

"I'm slowly taking the gun out of my waistband, okay? I'm not doing anything wrong, okay?" His pleading bounced off the officers and floated into the abyss.

"Do it now!"

Dre's right hand slowly disappeared behind his back and re-emerged with the gun. He pointed the weapon towards the steps, safely away from the officers.

"It's out. I'll put it down now, sir."

Buzzcut moved behind us while his partner stayed perpendicular. Their fingers teased the triggers of their guns.

Dre continued, "Okay, I'm cooperating. Okay, I'm lowering my gun, okay?" His voice crackled. He kept his eyes focused on the officer in front of us as he lowered the gun.

"Nice and easy, boy!"

"We will kill you if you make a move," Buzzcut yelled.

Dre bent down, the gun moments away from finding a resting spot on the step. As he slowly lowered his body, the mixture of nerves and the awkward position overpowered his usually graceful balance, and he lost his footing. His lower leg slipped a few inches and his body began to fall. He reached out for the metal railing with his left hand, trying to catch his fall. His right hand was positioned over the rail as his feet found steady ground, but he still had the gun in his hand. He still had the gun!

My eyes opened wide as the officers took a more defensive stance; their actions were automatic. Their fingers squeezed the triggers as if that was the only option. My body moved in a slow motion as I screamed, "WAITTTT."

But it was too late.

The shots were rapid and too quick to count. *Pop-pop.* The sound of fireworks rang throughout the neighborhood.

Pop-pop!

Pop-pop! Slowly, my hearing grew dull. I looked at the officers, and they stood there, guns still aimed, sweat glistening off their brows and the sense of *what just happened* appeared in their eyes.

My crimson-splashed hands trembled. They matched the rest of my body. My eyes slowly made their way to my brother, his body slumped over the steps, projecting blood like a geyser. There was no movement. No breathing. No cries of pain. Nothing. Just silence. My hero was dead.

Chapter 16

I opened my eyes.

"He slipped!"

My fists were balled up as my heart pounded through my chest. I repeated those words over and over again; Dre slipped. I tried to fight off the tears, but they flowed like heavy August rain. My parents grabbed me and held me tight. I could feel our heartbeats syncing; my father on my right, my mother on my left.

"And what about Jacob Zander?" Detective Berry's eyes now locked on mine.

Oh, Jake. I had forgotten about Jake.

"Before your brother's death, a fifteen-year-old boy was rushed to the hospital at roughly the same time. It was down the street from where the officers found you. Miracle, I'm not one to believe in coincidences, so, tell me," he demanded, "what about Jacob Zander?"

I didn't answer. I didn't know what to say.

I let out a soft whimper and buried my head in my hands. Thoughts of Jake lying face down in the dirt were permanently etched in my mind forever. Not even he deserved such a fate.

"That is enough!" my father shouted, springing out of his seat. "I think..." my dad stuttered, revealing his lack of confidence, "we should get a lawyer." He nodded to my mother, but she was staring off.

Detective Berry sighed. He leaned back in his chair and pondered for a brief second. "Very well." Detective Berry stood up, causing his chair to scrape against the floor. As he began walking out the door, he paused. He looked back. A sign of pity crossed his face. Then, he walked out.

Chapter 17

The sun peeked through the blinds, bringing the brightness of the day to reality. I flipped the sheet cover over my face hoping for the night to magically reappear, but my efforts were futile.

I dragged myself out of bed and staggered to the bathroom. The cool tiles chilled my body but did little to fully wake me. My hand fumbled its way, searching for the light switch. The brightness hit me like a thousand suns.

"What the hell?" I mumbled. My morning breath almost jolted me awake.

The reflection in the mirror revealed an unrecognizable version of me. My puffy blood-shot eyes squinted from the light as last night's pillow lines stretched across the left side of my face. I collected the loose strands of my braids and merged them with a neon-green hair band.

After a few splashes of cold water to my face, my eyes widened as I stood there staring at my reflection. My eyes seemed still. Calm. But inside, I knew the truth. I knew the harsh reality waiting for me beyond that bathroom door. It was the truth of yesterday, and it was real.

I headed into the kitchen. The emotional rollercoaster of the last few hours had left me void of any energy. I had to gain some kind of strength for whatever was to come. I wasn't that hungry, but the rumbling in my stomach said otherwise.

A handful of fruit sat on the counter, so I opted for an orange. I just stared at it for a few minutes, too lazy to unpeel it.

I gazed over the counter to see my parents awake, watching the television. The news was on in the background with a headline, "Lancaster PD fatally shoots Black teen: sparks riots." Images of protests had spread like wildfire, engulfing Lancaster and the nation. Black Lives Matter signs were held by mobs of people; some White, some Latino, but the majority Black. Marches led by celebrities shifted from one street to another, protesting for equal rights and the heads of the officers involved.

Looters were vandalizing police cars and neighboring stores. They weren't even wearing masks to hide their identities. This pain and anger had left them unable to think about the consequences of tomorrow.

The news reporter, a late-twenty-something white female, dressed as if she was in a combat zone, interviewed eyewitnesses. An older Black man shouted, "Well, these cops need to stop with the killing. It isn't right. Nah, this isn't right!"

One lady, maybe in her early thirties, with a sign that read, "This could have been my son!" yelled into the microphone with tears, "When will this end? When will the massacre of innocent Black men and women stop? Why must we be scared to go outside? Why must I tell my five-year-old son…." She paused momentarily to wipe the tears. "Why must I tell him what to do when a police officer approaches him? Why!?"

The interviews continued; they seemed like they were on a constant loop. The anger people felt was real, but I didn't understand why they were so angry. It was *my* brother who was killed. *My* brother.

My mom sat on the couch while my dad stood, their eyes glued to the screen. They didn't even realize I was there. I must have made a sound because my dad jumped, causing him to juggle the remote while trying to turn off the TV. My mother attempted to hide her tears, but it was obvious; no mother could hide those emotions. She wiped her face with the sleeve of her robe and gave her best attempts at greeting me with a smile.

"Good morning. How are you feeling?"

"I'm alright," I replied, looking down at my still untouched orange.

"We got a call from that detective this morning. He'd like us to come in for another interview," my dad said.

"Christ, Jesus," my mother mumbled, crossing her arms with discontent. She rocked back and forth, retreating into her own world.

"Do I have to go? I don't…." I couldn't finish the sentence. I didn't want to go for so many reasons. I didn't want to because I was tired and weak. I didn't want to because I was angry. I didn't want to because my mind was on an endless loop, replaying every moment of yesterday. But mainly, I didn't want to because I was afraid, afraid of what I might say.

"I don't want to because I'm tired," I finished. My dad walked over to me and rested his hands on my shoulders.

"Well, we have to, Bubble Gum. All you have to do is tell that guy what happened." He paused. "Whatever it is." He leaned in and wrapped his arms around me.

"I thought we needed a lawyer."

"A friend is hooking us up with one. She should meet us at the police station. So go get ready, okay?"

"Yes, sir."

He held me for a while, humming his favorite little melody in my ear.

I looked over at my mom. She continued to sit; her eyes zoned in on the television. She hunched over as she rocked back and forth. This was taking a toll on her, and it was apparent.

The morning quickly turned to the afternoon. My parents and I forced ourselves to get dressed to head back to the police department. Sluggish couldn't even describe how I felt. Every inch of my body felt heavy, hindering any forward progress in getting ready.

When we arrived, a few protesters lined the sidewalk in front of the building. And it wasn't just protesters; there were tons of news reporters from almost every major news agency. They hovered like vultures waiting for their prey, their cameras on standby and mics wired.

The sight of the people caused my body to go into immediate shock. The feeling of light-headedness rushed over me, leaving me frozen, unable to move forward. My father grabbed my hand and pulled me along with him. I managed to look up at him, and as I did, he mouthed the word, "Breathe!" With that one word as my armor of defense, we walked into the Lancaster Police Department, not knowing what would happen next.

Chapter 18

The police station was filled with people. Some were uniformed officers pushing handcuffed criminals to the backrooms. Other officers, likely detectives, wore suits as they typed away at their computers. The reflection of the monitors illuminated their tired faces.

My dad motioned for me and my mom to take seats in the waiting area. We found an empty row behind a mother who had three young kids in tow, all screaming and whining for their daddy. Against the wall sat an old man dressed in a U. S. Navy sweatshirt, with a black Vietnam Veteran hat perched on his head. A Times magazine rested on his lap as he squinted to read the text.

I looked up to see my dad talking to a woman at the front desk. They exchanged a handshake, and my dad nodded his head as she spoke. Then they turned to me and she gave me a smile.

The woman was rocking a dark grey blazer with matching pants, a white V-neck blouse, and black pumps. Her jewelry reeked of elegant simplicity. A rose gold bar necklace dangled on her chest as a matching rose gold bracelet wrapped around her right wrist. A thin black Fitbit hugged the other. Her hair was pulled into a French braid and her makeup was similar to her accessories, simple yet professional. Her look was topped off with giant, black-brimmed glasses.

The two approached.

"Hey, Miracle. I would like you to meet-"

"Courtney Bradley," I interrupted.

She smiled. "You can call me CB if you'd like."

Even in my foggy state, I knew who Courtney Bradley (I mean CB) was. She was like a real-life Black superhero. Well, more like a famous lawyer and advocate for equality and human rights.

She graduated at the top of her class at Howard University. She fought for justice and equality for the people, all the people, not just for Blacks. CB won the famous "Maryland vs. Acuna" trial, highlighting the injustice for disabled people in the hospitality industry. Then, she gained nationwide notoriety with her win in the "Nelson vs. Butler" case, fighting for the rights of low-income families in the education system. Of course, I knew who she was.

"CB has graciously volunteered to represent us during this process," my dad said. My mom stood up and shook her hand.

"This case will be very high profile. Cops shoot and kill a Black teen, again." CB shakes her head in sorrow. "I'm here to prepare you and your family for whatever legal actions arise."

I tried to smile, but the thought of legal actions was already too much for me to bear.

"My goal is simple; to help you and your family get the justice you deserve, simple as that." I nodded. "But first, let's get through today's questioning and we'll go from there. Sound good?" My parents nodded. I think we all braced ourselves, not knowing what was in store for us. For me.

Chapter 19

The questioning picked up where it left off the night before, but this time, CB joined us.

"My client, Miracle, and her family are willing to answer any additional questions you may have."

"Fair enough." Detective Berry smirked. "Let's talk about Jacob Zander." He paused to see my expression. My eyes widened as dread fell over me. "So, where would you like to start?"

I explained the burrito-throwing incident to the detective. I had to stop several times to let the information sink in for my parents. Their outrage was written on their faces and forever seared in their hearts.

"What did Dre do after they got out of the jeep?"

"Dre," I paused. I looked up at CB.

"It's okay. Go ahead."

I nodded. "Dre pointed the gun at Jake and Erik." My mother gasped. My father leaned forward, placing his hands over his face.

"He was scared. He thought they were going to kill us." I turned to my parents. "He was just protecting me. They had weapons."

"It's okay, Bubble Gum." My dad grabbed my hand and squeezed. Then, he nodded towards the detective and I turned back around.

"It's hard to believe it was self-defense. Dre had a gun while they had what?" Detective Berry looked over his notes. "A crowbar."

"No, I swear." I stood up. "He even said it. He said he feared for our lives."

"I would say a crowbar is pretty threatening. I can think of at least three crowbar-related deaths, Detective," CB chimed in.

Detective Berry nodded. He grabbed his pen and began to write while mumbling, "Self-defense."

"Where did he get the gun?"

I shrugged.

"I understand Andre was an associate of Rieko Ramirez." My eyes grew wide. Rieko. "Mr. Ramirez is a known member of the Grape Street Crips. They are known for running those streets. Was Andre a member? Maybe it was Mr. Ramirez who gave your brother the gun?"

"No." I wrinkled my face at the thought of Dre in a gang. "Absolutely not." My head shook frantically.

"Our son is," my dad paused, "was a good kid. He wasn't in a gang."

"Yeah, he wasn't," I said. I turned to CB as she patted her hands in the air. I took a deep breath and tried to calm myself.

The questioning continued, but from that point I was on autopilot. My heart ripped with every accusation, every question, every look. I felt the detective didn't want to hear my side of the story. He didn't want the truth. All he wanted was to clear his officers and label another Black man as a criminal.

After what seemed like hours, we heard rumblings outside the room. Detective Berry excused himself to investigate the noise. My father rubbed my back and whispered, "It'll be over soon and then we can go home." I looked up into his coffee-brown eyes and nodded.

"You're doing great, Miracle," CB said.

"Thanks." I hung my head down, exhausted.

After several minutes, Detective Berry rushed back in.

"Sorry about that. Listen, we'll have to continue this interview another time." He quickly rushed us out the door. "Please do not speak to anyone." At this point, he stared directly at me. "And I mean ANYONE about what happened."

"My client already knows not to discuss this with anyone outside of the investigation," CB assured the detective. She extended her hand, and the detective returned the gesture.

Detective Berry motioned for us to take the back entrance of the police department. "This may be safer for you. Good night, and I'll call you tomorrow."

"You guys go ahead. I'll call tomorrow. I want to stay behind and check on some things."

"Thanks for everything, CB. Glad you're on our side," my dad said.

She shot my parents a smile and turned to me.

"You really did a great job today. I'll stop by in a few days." With that, she headed back inside the police station as we headed out the back door.

Detective Berry's comment hung in my head. *This may be safer for you.* I didn't understand his comment until we slid out the back of the station and rounded the corner of the street where the police department's entrance was located.

The small group of protesters and reporters we passed earlier had transformed into hundreds of people. Protestors stood carrying signs and shouting at the top of their lungs, "No justice, no peace! No justice, no peace!"

They all stood there, eyeing the police department, tears flowing down their cheeks and anger filling their hearts. Their yells were directed at the police department. Still, in reality, we all knew it was directed at something bigger than just the Lancaster PD.

To them, this was just another tragic event, which led to the murder of another young Black person destined to be someone greater than just a statistic.

In 2020, our country was filled with riots and protests that shook the core of our nation. The tipping point took place earlier this year, with the death of Mechelle Williams.

Mechelle was a twenty-three-year-old government employee who was pulled over, dragged out of her car, and choked unconscious by two very junior police officers, all because the police officers said she fit the description of a Black forty-seven-year-old drug dealer.

At first, there was little in the media about that case until the LA County coroner's office published the autopsy report. Mechelle had been four months pregnant at the time of her death. It wasn't surprising when the public wanted justice and revenge.

Our city was on lockdown for weeks. No one was allowed to go outside: no work, no school, no nothing. That was when my parents gave me "the talk."

This talk did not involve sex. This was the talk passed down from generation to generation but is hardly spoken about in public forums. It was about the harsh reality of surviving in a world that sees people of color as inferior, having to do twice the work as our white counterparts. As my parents explained, we had to fight for everything we ever wanted in life; whether for our education, our job, or our family. We had to fight! The talk was supposed to be a wake-up call to always be on the alert, but for Dre and me, it stood as a constant reminder that equal rights didn't exist. At least, not here.

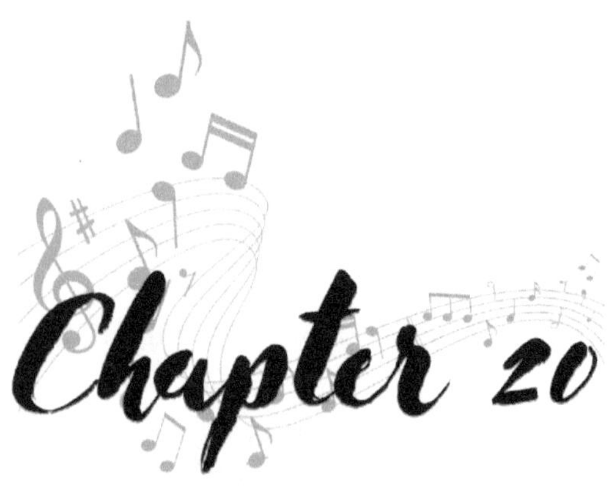

Chapter 20

My father rushed us to the car, hoping not to get mixed up in the excitement. We all knew if anyone recognized us, we'd be swarmed by protesters and reporters aching for an update. After all, it was my brother who was killed.

Luckily, our car was parked down the street, away from the commotion. We quickly jumped into our waiting Nissan Altima. I buckled up and sunk into my seat.

The silence in the car was deafening. Even the radio remained off as our bodies gently bounced around the seats, dodging one blocked road after another. Streetlights flickered through the window as police sirens echoed in the background. Flashes of red and orange broke through the glass as I stared out the window. Our precious little city was engulfed in flames and violence.

Pedestrians stood in front of stores, watching in shock as looters threw trash cans into storefront windows. A gaggle of teens rushed out of a local electronics store, carrying boxes filled with TVs and radios. My eyes spotted an older Black man waving a bat in the face of would-be looters, trying to ward off damage to his store. An Asian man cowered over his family, looking in disbelief as monstrous flames shot out from inside his restaurant.

"What is this world coming to?" My dad shook his head in disbelief, watching a world gone mad. How can anyone justify such destruction in honor of Dre's memory?

Mom remained silent, staring out the window. I wondered what she was thinking.

The scene was too unbearable. I reached for my headphones and tried to drown out the world. With a simple tap on the small display, the music began. I closed my eyes and leaned my head against the window, my arm acting as a pillow.

As the music built, my pulse reverberated through the headphones. My heart was elevated, which wouldn't surprise anyone, considering recent events. The song began. Willow Marie's soulful voice radiated through the headphones and landed in my heart. I took a breath. Then another.

Suddenly, my fingers began to tingle. Goosebumps sprouted across my arms and a familiar cold feeling rushed over me once again. This time, I didn't resist. I yearned for an escape from the reality of the night. I opened myself up, and then the falling feeling took over, followed by darkness.

Chapter 21

The darkness vanished as my eyes slowly slid open and I took in the scene. A soft cloud of cigarette smoke hung in the air, resting over folks engaged in rousing conversations. Embellished laughter ensued in the background as a feeling of excitement and exhilaration lingered throughout the dark-lit bar.

Photos of musicians hung along the red draped walls; a saxophone player in one frame, a drummer in another. Small round tables scattered across the wooden floor while dim candles illuminated the center of each table, casting a sensual shadow upon the patrons.

Some men wore dark suits with matching folded brim hats, while others rocked white button-down shirts. Scarfs slung over their shoulders as suspenders pressed against their torsos and ties kissed their necks. The women looked luxurious with their hair pinned up and their dresses pressed tightly against their curvy bodies. Their bright painted lips screamed for attention.

Suddenly, the bar lights lowered and a soft light emerged in the middle of the stage. It was a small oval-shaped stage with only enough room for a microphone stand and a beautiful black grand piano. A man hidden in the shadows sat at the piano, his fingers resting on the keys.

The room erupted with applause as a slim young Black woman stepped from the darkness to take center-stage. Her curly black hair flowed over her shoulders and rested on the right corner of a beautiful red dress with a long slit on the right side. Her hands wrapped around the microphone, revealing long bright red nails that matched her dress.

As her lips parted, a hush fell over the crowd. She closed her eyes and hit the first note, then the second. We sat, entranced by her voice, unable to take our eyes off her.

> "Uplift me and make me float away,
> like an evergreen.
> Kiss me and make my soul melt away."

I found a stool at the bar in the back of the club and watched in amazement.

> "Stay, please, my darling, stay.
> Let's cherish these times.
> Let's cherish these days.
> My darling, please stay."

A tear raced down my face, and then another as she continued. My hand slid across my cheek, but it was pointless; the tears kept coming. I tried to hide my emotions, but I noticed I wasn't alone. Others hid their tears, while the brave let themselves feel the emotion. The tears mixed in with their eyeliner, causing small black rivers to flow down their cheeks.

After her last note, she stepped back from the microphone. The crowd immediately sprung from their chairs, letting out a thunderous roar. The singer took a humble bow and then motioned to her piano player. The crowd continued pounding their hands together, outdone by whistles and a few shouts of appreciation.

With one final kiss to the crowd, she slowly and elegantly walked off the stage. Heck, even her walk was angelic. She floated along the floor, passing men and women who were still clapping. Their compliments continued, met with a humble yet sincere smile.

Before I knew it, she stood next to me and stuck a finger out to the bartender. Understanding her secret code, he pushed a glass of water to the singer; a small slice of lemon buried under three ice cubes. I had wiped my tears away by this time and tried my best to compose myself.

"You were amazing," I mumbled with a shaky voice.

"Thank ya, darling. Neva seen you 'round here before."

"Yeah, I'm new here."

"Well, New Here, I'm Darlene."

"Miracle… My name is Miracle."

"Miracle, so what are you running away from?"

My eyes grew big and I shot her a puzzled look.

"Darlin', the only time folks come 'round here to the Victoria is when they escapin' from somethan'.'" She leaned forward. "Child, look 'round. These folks come here to run away…from their spouses, jobs, and lives. The Victoria is where ya go to feel free."

My eyes glanced over the crowd. "But they all seem happy."

"Yeah, they look as happy as a dead pig in the sunshine, suga. But that doesn't mean they are. So…" Darlene leaned closer in and placed her hand on my shoulder. She smelled of lavender. "Whatcha runnin' from, child?"

"Death…" She gripped me a little tighter. "My brother died yesterday and I…."

There was a long pause. Darlene didn't press me to continue; she just waited. At this point, my tears reappeared, and there was no stopping them.

Darlene turned to the bartender and requested another glass of water. He obliged.

"Drink some wata, suga'. Ya know, nothin' I can say is going to make that pain go 'way. Hell, it may neva go way, child. But my momma once told me that death is the final journey of life and everyone needs to end their journey."

The water was cold. I looked up from my glass and wiped my tears away, but they kept coming.

"You goin' be a'ight, suga…and if not, you can always come back to the Victoria and just ask for ya friend Darlene."

My cheeks stretched out into a half smile and I looked up at her. She gave me a soft smile in return and then, she was gone.

When we got home, my father pulled into our garage. I was so grateful to be home finally. I slid between the car and the narrow passageway with several shelves of boxes marked "photo albums" on the other side. Once I walked in, my dad turned to me. His blood-shot eyes met mine, and he said, "It'll be okay, Bubble Gum." I stared into his eyes once again and collapsed in his arms.

Chapter 22

The next few days were filled with a lot of tears and silence. We all handled Dre's death differently. I barely left my bedroom. My parents, realizing I needed time, gave me my space.

They delivered cooked meals to my bedroom door. My father would check on me, but he was met with rejection each time, either through a cold shoulder or through the silent treatment. Eventually, I pretended to be asleep when I heard him walking towards my room. It seemed easier than constantly brushing him and the rest of the world off.

My parents didn't handle his death any easier. They grew up in the south as children of Civil Rights activists, so they were familiar with loss. Unfortunately, no loss can compare to that of a child, your child. My dad tried to stay strong for the family, but mom often saw him crying to himself in the garage when he thought no one was looking. He would never allow himself to cry in front of us.

My mom took it the worst. She became distant and more sheltered. We didn't know it at the time, but she would never be the same again. I guess none of us would.

Almost a year later, my parents would split up. My dad couldn't save their relationship and opted to fight for me instead of his wife. I couldn't blame him. I couldn't blame either one of them. When death hits you, you never really know how you'll react. But we'll save that conversation for later.

Kim kept calling and texting to make sure I was okay:

"Hey, uh… Are you okay? No, that's a dumb question. Can we talk?"

"Hey, Miracle, I miss you. Can we talk?"

"I just wanted to say that…I…I mean…just call me."

"Everyone at school misses you. Want me to come over? We can have a sleepover."

"Greg and Autumn wanted to say hi, and…just call me."

It was Kim who actually broke me from my cocoon of silence. A voice message she left (actually, one of twenty-four voice messages she left) made me snap back into reality.

"Hey, Miracle, I know you're in pain, and you're ghosting everyone. But Dre was my family, too. You're my family!"

After listening to her message, I sent her a text saying I was okay and then I finally emerged from my cave. My parents were in the kitchen having a conversation. They stopped when I walked in, not because I wasn't supposed to hear what they said but because they didn't know how to respond to my presence. I said my good mornings, even though it was sometime in the late afternoon and proceeded to pour myself a glass of water. Then our lives began once again.

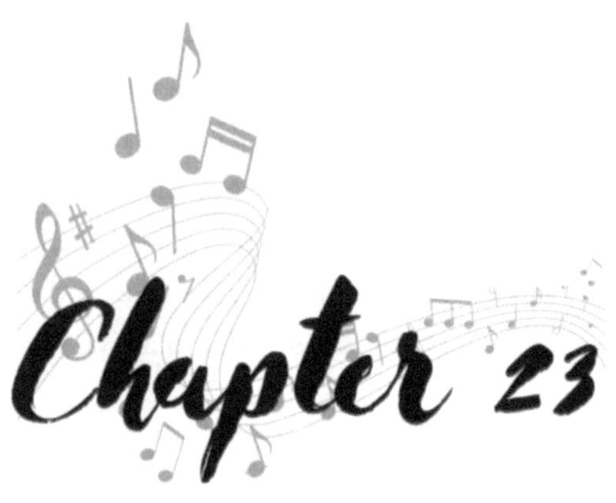

Chapter 23

I heard footsteps approach as I lay on my bed covered in crumbs and empty candy wrappers. Thinking my dad was about to check on me like he usually did, I slung my legs over the bed. I could hear the sound of crinkling as my right foot smashed an empty Dorito bag.

"Gross."

I rubbed my feet against the carpet, sending loose bits of chips flying from the bottom of my feet. I stood up as gentle tapping came from the door.

It was my dad. But this time, he wasn't alone.

"Bubble Gum, you have company."

My eyebrows rose as I tilted my head to see over his shoulder.

"Is it okay if they..." Before my dad could finish Autumn barged in, followed by Kim, while Greg remained next to my dad. In a flash Autumn and Kim wrapped me in their arms. I gasped. I wasn't sure what a broken rib felt like, but I was pretty sure those two ladies just broke a couple of them. Greg and my dad stood awkwardly in the doorway.

"I'll leave you to it, I guess." My dad gently pushed Greg into the room and slowly closed the door.

As the two released me from their kung fu grips, I took in a breath.

"Are you okay?" Autumn asked. "What can we do? Want me to rough those cops up?"

I allowed myself to smile for the first time since Dre's death.

"No, just make a vlog about it."

"Already did. Three, to be precise."

"Of course, you did."

Autumn smiled. I turned to Kim. She held her head down and shifted around on my bed. Her fingers twirled a strand of her auburn hair.

"Kim?"

Her beautiful blue eyes found mine. I smiled again, but it wasn't returned. Instead, Kim quickly bit down on her bottom lip as her body began to tremble. She let out a soft whimper. Then, her head collapsed in her hands as she started bawling. Tears seeped through her fingers.

My arms reached out, pulling her into me. She buried her head in my shoulder and wrapped her arms around my body. I squeezed, and she did the same. We both tried to take each other's pain away. We tried to do something to heal the other. After all, she lost a brother, too.

After a few minutes, our bodies disengaged. I stared into Kim's eyes as she did the same. My thumbs ran across her cheeks, wiping away her tears.

She let out a deep breath and shook her head. I mirrored her and shot her a slight smile.

Then, the room grew silent. No one knew quite what to say next. I put my head down, trying to build the courage to say something, anything, but nothing came out.

"We miss you, Miracle." We turned our heads to see Greg still standing where my dad had pushed him, seemingly too afraid to move further into my room. His eyes were focused on his shoes as he shifted his weight from one foot to the other. He looked up and shined his gentle smile.

I looked him in his eyes and then I lowered my head and began to cry.

My body shut down as the emotion took over. All the pain, heartbreak, and sadness rushed over me, and there was nothing I could do to stop it. My heart ached as if a thousand knives suddenly stabbed me. I clutched my chest as my body folded over.

"Why…" I screamed out.

Suddenly, the warmth of an embrace blanketed me. It was Kim and then Autumn.

"Why!" I blubbered.

They squeezed me even tighter, our tears now running parallel.

"Shhhh," Autumn whispered.

"I'm so sorry," Kim mumbled between tears. The shaking of our bodies made it almost impossible to understand. Greg's eyes watered. He wiped a few tears and turned away.

We sat wrapped in each other's arms for maybe minutes, hours, days even, I wasn't sure, but the feeling of their embrace and love shielded me from the pain. I still felt the pain, but it was different now. Eventually, tears were replaced by words and then smiles. The tears found their way back several times, but they were always met with more group hugs.

"So, this is what your room looks like?" asked Greg as he studied my bedroom. Sweatpants and t-shirts were slung over a chair and worn socks were scattered around the room. Used Kleenexes and empty soda bottles covered my desk. I could only imagine what I looked like, or worse, smelled like. I suddenly realized I hadn't left or cleaned my room for a week.

Embarrassed, I said, "I swear, it's not always like this." Greg's eyebrows sprung up as his mocha-brown cheeks grew a rosy hue. I traced his eyes to find my red poke-a-dot bra slung over the chair.

"Oh, I didn't mean it like that…I mean…" He stumbled nervously, trying to find the right words. The girls and I just giggled at his embarrassment.

After a few hours, I walked my friends to the door. It was getting late and I desperately needed a shower. Kim gave me a monstrous hug. I could hear and feel a few of my ribs breaking. *How the hell is that little girl so strong?* I wondered. Autumn and I said our goodbyes as well.

Greg gave me a fist bump, our usual goodbye, and wished me a good night. As I closed the door, I felt resistance on the other side. A hand appeared, pushing the door open. It was Greg. I opened the door wider and he leaned in and wrapped his arms around me.

The hug was a pleasant surprise. His cheeks felt soft against mine and had a sweet smell. It reminded me of Halloween night, after trick-or-treating with Dre and unloading all of our chocolate on the dining room table.

Greg whispered, "When I heard the news, I thought I'd never see you again." I squeezed tighter. His heart raced against my chest. As he let go, he locked his eyes on mine and said, "If you ever need anything, I'll always be here for you." His eyes were comforting.

I placed my hand on his chest. "Thank you."

As he walked away, he suddenly turned back.

"Always."

My heart felt reassured as if for a moment, everything would be alright.

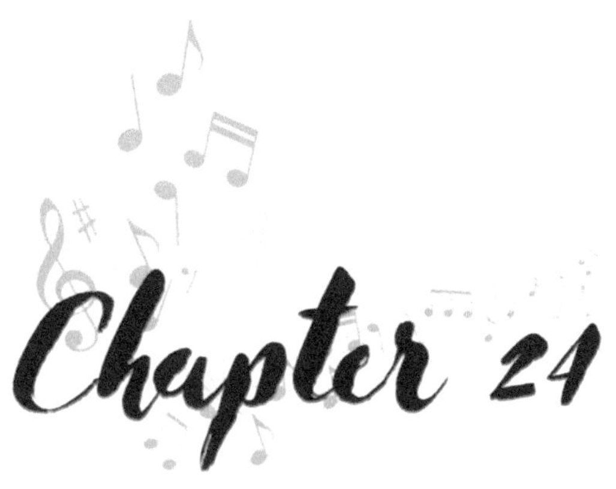

Chapter 24

Days turned to weeks, and the rest of the world moved on, but one thing remained. Kim and Autumn sat on the edge of my bed. I was sprawled on the floor, laying on some oversized pillows that were usually reserved for décor. Greg shoved his hands down a Dorito bag as he sat in my fluffy pink chair in the corner.

I was getting accustomed to our new daily routine; my friends coming to my apartment to fill me in on the outside world. Greg would bring my schoolwork each day, and Autumn would always show me her latest podcast, which lately, was focused on the protests. I would update them on preparations with CB.

That night, we were sitting in my room watching the news showing footage of the riots days after my brother's death. Videos displayed people of every age, race, and background flooding the streets, blocking cars, and throwing anything not nailed down. A female news reporter, Meghan Clooney, rattled off questions for her three guests.

"These officers were outnumbered and weren't equipped to handle this type of situation," roared a frumpy older man. The caption read Bruce Lennings, Former Chicago Police Chief.

"Nothing can sway the people's hunger for justice," cracked a younger Black woman, her micro-braids slung over her long-sleeve black midi dress. It was CB.

"Let's go CB," Kim cheered.

"Woohoow," Greg yelled.

"We've seen it following the senseless death of George Floyd in 2020," she adjusted her dark brimmed glasses resting on the edge of her nose, "and we see it now. The people want justice! The family needs justice."

"We need to do something," Autumn jumped from the bed, waving her arms.

"Like what?" Greg asked. He rubbed his hands along the arms of the pink faux fur chair.

"I don't know. We should be out there, fighting for the people, for your brother." She stopped as her attention went back to the news footage.

"How would us going out there help anyone?" Kim asked. "Plus, the riots have died down. There are barely any protesters anymore."

"You wouldn't get it, Kim. This isn't about you."

Suddenly, the room grew cold. Greg's eyes widened and my jaw dropped.

"Excuse me? What does that mean?" Kim furrowed her eyebrows and tilted her head. Then she stood up.

I looked over at Greg. He shot me a quick glance and then his eyes slowly focused on the bottom of the empty chip bag.

Autumn sighed. "You. Wouldn't. Get. It!" She annunciated every word. "I'm not sure if you noticed, but this war…this injustice," she said as she stretched out her arm, pointing to the television, "is happening to *my* people." She motioned to Greg and then me. "*Our* people."

"Oh my God." Kim shook her head in frustration. "You barely even knew Dre. He was like a brother to me."

Autumn stepped closer to Kim, standing nose to nose. "Well, he *was* my brother."

Her eyes locked on Kim's. Kim clenched her jaw. This was a new side of Kim.

Autumn's breath grew shallower as Kim stood void of motion. The sound of the news faded in the background as the silence grew. Suddenly, laughter interrupted the silence, bringing the opponents back to reality. We all turned to find Greg laughing hysterically. We all stared.

"What are you…." I gestured.

He chuckled before I could finish. "She said, 'he's my brother, too.' He reached for his stomach as if in pain. "My brother, too," he continued. The girls looked at me and I shrugged. However, his laughter grew infectious, and before I knew it, I joined in.

Kim relaxed her face and sat back on the bed. She took a few deep breaths, trying to calm herself down.

Autumn folded her arms, throwing daggers at us. She sighed heavily, "Whatever!" She sat back on the bed, shoulder to shoulder with Kim, and turned her attention back to the television.

The laughter faded and silence once again filled the air. After a few moments, Autumn broke her silence.

"Our people," she began, "have been held down by your people for decades."

All heads turned to Autumn.

"Let me guess," Kim said, "because of slavery?"

"Slavery! It has held us back. I feel like I'm still in chains. But you wouldn't get it because of your…white privilege."

"What white privilege?"

"Can we not do this?" I tried to defuse the situation, to no avail.

"What white privilege?! What white privilege?"

Autumn jumped from the bed again. "Girl, you have to be tripping. We have to struggle twice as hard as you to succeed in life. We are paid less. We are denied access to proper education in schools. We…"

"I'm fine in school," Greg interrupted. More daggers. "Just saying. Uh, never mind. I'm good. Please continue."

"Anyways," Autumn continued. Kim let her speak, but I could see steam fuming from her ears. "You get more chances to succeed and are expected to succeed. All people want from me is to stay at the bottom. No fancy cars, no high-paying career. Just po lil black girl trying to do her black girl magic with fifteen cents." Her head bounced side to side as her hands waved in the air. "This is why we need to fight. This is why there are riots. Justice!" She pounded her fist into her hand. "Peace!" Another fist to the hand. "Racial equality!" The final fist hit like a judge's gavel.

Kim slumped her shoulders and stared at her shoes. Autumn smirked. "Mmhmm." She panned over at us. I shook my head. Greg did the same.

A soft voice broke the silence. "What privileges do I have, Autumn?" She took a breath. "I don't have a cushy life. I never have. My father works two jobs and still struggles to put food on the table. My mom," she paused, stared off and then continued. "Every good thing that has ever happened in my life was filled with nothing...NOTHING," she said as she curled her hand into a ball, "but heartache and worry. Worried the lights won't get paid or dad will lose his job or..." she paused, "we'll have to live in our car again."

I had no idea. How could I not have known?

"We are poor." Her eyes began to water, but she didn't allow herself to cry; not in front of Autumn.

"I'm sorry, Miss Kim, but what the hell does this have to do with the injustices we as Black people face daily?"

"Are you kidding..." Kim began but was interrupted.

"The twin of racial injustice is economic injustice." We glanced over at Greg. "Martin Luther King said that." We all stared. "Well, he did." He shrugged.

I shot him a smile as he ran his fingers through the pink fabric. He never failed to surprise me.

"Just saying, Black people have been victims since we got here, but so have the poor. Jails aren't just filled with us. They are filled with poor Hispanics and poor White people, too," Greg continued. "So, yes, life is hard as a Black man or woman, but it's not so easy for others, either."

I nodded my head in agreement.

"Whatever," Autumn huffed.

"I'm not saying what Black people go through shouldn't be fixed. We all know it should. But I can't let you stand here and complain about those same problems when you are the reason for most of the problems you have."

Autumn's head snapped in Kim's direction. Standing inches away, she asked, "Excuse me? Oh, it's my fault?"

"Yes, Autumn, it's your fault!" The hostility on the television paled in comparison to the tension in my bedroom.

"No one can use you as a poster child for suffering."

"And what does that mean?"

"You're from a great family. Heck, your parents are doctors and they're still together, which is awesome, but..."

"I can't help it if your dad couldn't keep your mom. That has nothing to do with..."

"My mom is dead!" Her voice shook as her body tensed.

Autumn raised her eyebrows and she quickly glanced at me. I gave her a gentle nod to confirm and she looked back at Kim. I could see Autumn's eyes scanning the floor, trying to figure out the right words to salvage this moment.

The room went silent. I had never seen Kim so…so raw and vulnerable. Autumn didn't reply. Kim took several deep breaths, still staring at the floor.

"Do you think Dre would be alive if he were white?"

Autumn sat with a smug look on her face. She stared at Kim as she patiently waited for a response. My head was swimming, my thoughts screaming with anger. I closed my eyes and took in a deep, deliberate breath. On the exhale, my body trembled with rage. Kim finally looked up, and her lips parted.

Before her voice could take over, I sprung from the floor.

"I can't... not right now, not ever. I simply can't."

I stormed out of the room, slamming the door behind me.

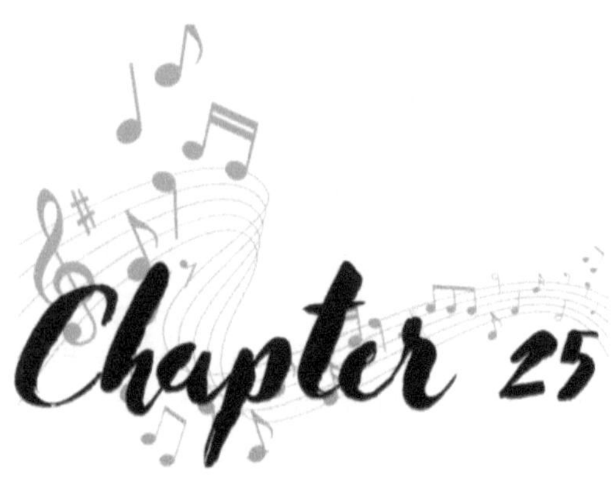

Chapter 25

It was the one-month anniversary of my brother's death. Although my heart was still fractured and my mind whirled with emotions, I knew I couldn't hide forever. It was time to return to school. My dad supported my decision and my mom, well, she just nodded off in space every time I brought it up. Guess her mind was more messed up than mine.

Since Dre's death, the school was gracious enough to place me in a weird stay-at-home schedule. Greg was kind enough to bring me most of my assignments and then I would turn them in online. This was reminiscent of the big Corona virus scare that took over the world several years prior. It savaged the globe, killing more than four million people, forcing everyone to shelter in their homes; thus, the online learning wave. Kids loved it. Parents hated it.

The virus's origin was never fully explained. Still, our government said it came from people in China eating bats. Greg always thought it was cultivated by evil scientists who wanted to weaken other countries to start their own invasion of robot soldiers. Did I mention Greg was a huge sci-fi nerd? Yeah, if it wasn't evil scientists, it was the zombies. Those darn zombies.

Secretly, I was using going back to school as another way to connect with other people. My daily routine of my three friends coming over quickly dwindled away. The tension between Autumn and Kim grew too strong; even though they did try to be polite for my sake. However, each time one or the other ended up storming out. Eventually, Kim slowly stopped coming over and then Autumn did the same. Greg kept coming over until my dad put an end to that. He wasn't a fan of his precious daughter being alone in a room with a boy, especially a boy that was the same height as him.

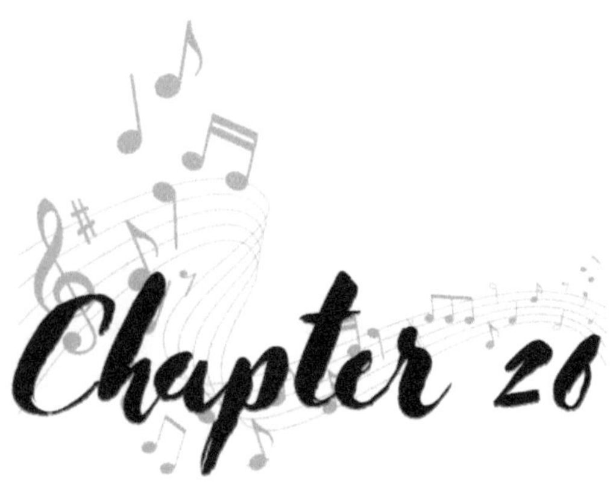

Chapter 26

When my dad opened the door CB walked in carrying a Chloe white purse that matched her high heels. A black laptop bag and a stainless-steel cyan water bottle accessorized her light grey business suit and pants; professional yet sporty.

She was followed by a man wearing a navy-blue suit with a pink tie and black shoes. He was older, maybe in his 50s. His brown hair was slowly being drowned by grey. A gold ring rested on his wedding finger and a smile adorned his face. His eyes seemed kind, kind blue eyes.

They stepped in and my parents greeted them.

"Miracle, this is Richard Greene," CB said.

"I'll be the prosecutor in the trial."

"Oh, I thought CB was our lawyer."

"I am." CB smiled. "We're sort of like a packaged deal; two for the price of one."

Mr. Greene smiled. "That's an interesting way of putting it."

"Sounds good to me."

"I've known Richard for years. Trust me; we definitely want him on our side." Mr. Greene's cheeks flushed. A genuine smile stretched across his face.

"We'll make sure you're ready to testify when its time."

"Testify? Wait, she has to testify? Why does she have to testify?"

Mr. Greene's smile quickly vanished. "Sir, besides the police officers, she's the only one who can tell the world what really happened." He turned to me. "I would love to say we can achieve our goals without you taking the stand," he paused, "but the truth may never come out without you."

My dad nodded, and my mom sat motionless. She gazed off in the distance. My dad rubbed my mom's back, shaking her from her trance. Sadly, I had grown used to this sight.

"Okay, yeah, that's fine." Her reaction was somewhat robotic.

"Our job is simple. We will prepare you for what to expect, but please understand, it will not be easy. You must relive that day, every moment of it, because they will ask you about every single moment." At this point, Mr. Greene examined my face to see if I was still following him. I nodded.

"If it's okay with you," CB stopped and looked back at my parents, "and your parents, we'd like to begin this weekend."

"Okay, that's fine with us. Bubble Gum?"

"Yeah, cool. That's fine."

CB clasped her hands together. "Very well then. We'll get through this together and Mr. Greene and I will be here if you need anything." CB glanced at her counterpart who shook his head in agreement. "Okay, Ms. Miracle?"

"Yes…yes, ma'am."

My parents continued talking to the two lawyers while I stepped into my bedroom. I collapsed on my bed and stared at the ceiling. I rubbed the back of my neck and noticed my hands were shaking. I knew this emotional rollercoaster was about to get a lot bumpier.

Out of instinct, I reached for my phone and texted Kim. As usual, she called immediately.

"So, what are you going to do?"

"What can I do? I just hope I don't screw this up. I mean, it's a big deal. What if…"

She interrupted my rant, "Breathe, Miracle. We'll get through this together." CB had said those exact words. "We'll get through this together." I didn't know which was more comforting, having CB in my corner or Kim.

"You okay?" Kim asked, interrupting the silence.

I reflected on the people on my team; CB, Mr. Greene, Kim, Greg, my dad, and my heart filled with warmth. Suddenly, a gentle calm rushed over me. "Yeah, I'll be fine."

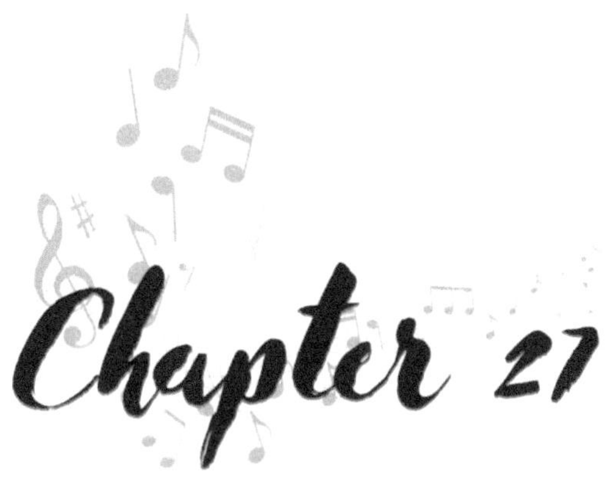

Chapter 27

The weekend quickly arrived and CB was already knocking on our door. After saying hello to my parents, she greeted me with a smile. "Ready to get started?"

"Let's do it."

I pulled out my usual chair at the dinner table and she sat opposite me. Within a flash, our dinner table transformed into a full-on operations center containing her Dell laptop, a small recording device, three mechanical pencils and a notepad. Her final item was a red bag of Skittles. I stared at the candy. She leaned in and said, "A girl can't be all business, right?" And with that we got started.

Her explanation of the trial was similar to going to the dentist. You know it'll be good for you, but the whole adventure scares you. She walked me through the various stages of the trial, the main players, and what types of questions could be asked. Yeah, I preferred going to the dentist.

"So, Andre killed Jacob, and now you expect me to believe he didn't try to kill the cops?"

I shot up from my desk. Anger leaked from my pores. "What the hell, CB?!"

She raised her hands in defense. "The other team will try to rile you up. I'm just trying to prepare you for what they may say. I do not think Andre was a bad guy. I promise." I sat back on the chair and folded my arms.

CB took a sip from her water bottle and stared at me. My eyes didn't meet hers. Instead, they found refuge on the clock that hung on the wall. The battery had died months before, but my dad never replaced it. It was stuck on 11:11.

"How about we take a break?" CB suggested. She reached for her Skittles and ripped open the bag.

"Okay."

Her hand slid across the table with a handful of colored treats. I reached out my hand and took a few. We sat there in silence as we chewed the refreshing candy.

"When I was younger,' she started, interrupting the silence, "I was supposed to give a speech to my class. Everyone was. It was for our end-of-semester grade, and I was so nervous." She paused and tossed a few more Skittles in her mouth.

"I spent weeks practicing in my bathroom mirror. Each time was worse than the time before. I was horrible." She let out a little giggle, recalling her lousy performance. "But guess what happened when the day finally came?"

"You crushed it. That's not surprising," I said, acting like I had heard this motivational speech before.

"Nope, I never had a chance."

"Wait. What?"

"Every kid before me was so bad that the teacher canceled the rest of the class." CB laughed. "One kid was so bad," CB paused to control her laughter, "she threw up in front of the entire classroom." Her laughter caused her eyes to shut as her body bounced up and down with every chuckle.

"Glad I didn't sit in the front row of that class," she concluded. Her body gyrated as a snort came out. And then another. She looked up as her thumb wiped away her tears. I sat and stared until, eventually, I joined in. We sat there for what seemed like hours, just laughing. It wasn't even funny, but I couldn't help myself. It reminded me of Kim and me; two girls laughing at nothing in particular.

"The point is," she composed herself and continued, "I spent all that time stressing myself out for absolutely nothing."

"No offense, CB, but that was a horrible motivational speech." She nodded, and our laughter continued.

Later that night, my finger scrolled through the various contacts on my phone until I reached Kim's avatar. It was an image of Velma from Scooby-Doo. My finger hung over her picture, but I didn't press it. Instead, I kept scrolling.

"Whatcha doing?"

"Nada, you?"

"Nothing, just sat down with CB. I'm freaking out."

"Why? You, okay?"

"I have a bad feeling about this trial."

A GIF of a bulldog with giant crying eyes and the words "SO SAD" popped up on my screen.

"Lol. Are you saying I look like a dog?"

"Lol. No. But now that you mention it…"

"And this is why you're single!"

Three dots appeared on the screen. Then, they disappeared.

I quickly typed, "I was just kidding."

"I know. And I'm single because I'm just waiting for you to say yes."

"Whatever, Greg, that'll never happen," I texted.

More three dots. Then, again, they disappeared.

"JK, sheesh. Quit being so sensitive. Plus, you can't be mad at me. You know you luvvv some Miracle."

I waited for his reply. Nothing. Moments later, I looked down and smiled. His response threw me back to the first night my three amazing friends came over. The night was rough, but laughter and friendship emerged victorious through the tears and pain. And when the night ended, Greg's words remained.

"Always!"

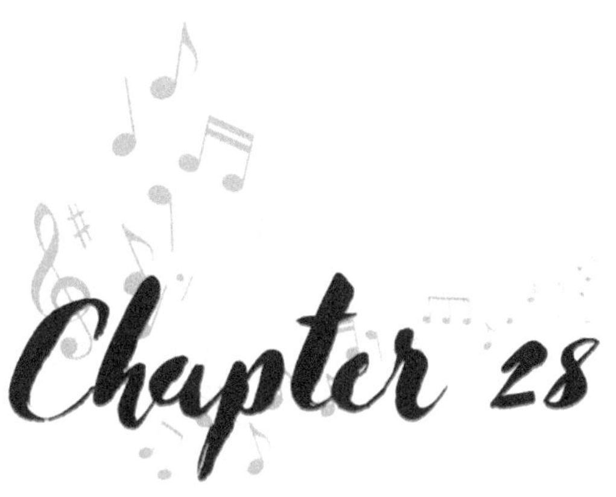

Chapter 28

Autumn blew us a kiss as she rounded the corner heading to her next class. We started walking away, and like clockwork, Greg tripped over his own two feet. The impact of his fall sent his papers, books, and a folder hurling in the air. I let out a little giggle and then made sure he was okay. Realizing there was no blood, he smiled and said, "I'm okay."

When will this kid ever learn to walk? I asked myself, struggling to lift his 6'2 frame, and together we began collecting his belongings. Other kids staggered past us, trying to avoid stepping on his papers. Some were successful. Others were not. I scooped up one of his loose papers, which now had a size 10 shoe imprint on it. I shot him a smile.

As the last of the fallen items were collected, we both stood in unison. I went over to hand him his stuff, and before I knew it, his lips pressed against mine. His lips were soft and warm to the touch. They tasted like cinnamon. The sweet aroma of his cheeks floated in the air. His teeth gently tapped against mine. A tab of drool slithered from his tongue to my bottom lip sending shivers down my spine.

Breaking my shock, I pulled away from him and stood there, frozen. My feet were unable to move. My heart thumped in my chest while my mouth remained slightly ajar. I let out the final breath in my lungs and stared into his deep brown eyes.

As we stood less than a foot away from each other, my eyes reflected his. He began to fidget. Before thinking of what to say, he mumbled, "I'm sorry," and quickly raced around the corner. I stood there, paralyzed by a thunderstorm of emotion.

Gross. That was the only word that I could think of. Greg kissed me. My thoughts touched down like a hurricane. He crossed a line that I wasn't ready to be crossed.

The school bell rung, breaking my frozen state. As I walked to my next class, I had just one thought: *That was my first kiss.*

The rest of the day was somewhat of a blur. I couldn't concentrate on any of my classes and kept to myself. Greg and I didn't speak. I think he tried a few times, but he scattered like leaves in a windstorm once our eyes met.

"What's up with Greg? He didn't hang out at lunch, and now," Kim gestured to the front of the bus, "he's sitting up there. It's like he's been avoiding us all day."

I shrugged her question off and focused my gaze out the window. Students passed by, heading to their cars. It was mainly the seniors and some juniors. Others had to ride the bus, like me, or wait until their parents came to pick them up.

My phone sent vibrations shooting through my hoody pocket. There was a text message waiting, and it read: "I lied to you. I'm not sorry!"

My eyes shot up. Greg wasn't sorry about the kiss.

The thought brought goosebumps to my arms as a cool sensation flowed over me. A giant smile crossed my face as I leaned against the window. I slid my earbuds in and closed my eyes, still smiling. Darkness.

Chapter 29

Through the darkness, the sound of one singular strum of a guitar hung in the air, then another. I opened my eyes to find myself sitting on an old wooden dock. My legs dangled over the wooden platform as flies buzzed across my head. The cool breeze of the water brushed against my cheeks as the sweet smell of nearby flowers filled the air.

I turned to take in my surroundings. To my right stood a forest with big beautiful mature trees and tall grass that lay at the foot of the trees. In front of me was a modest lake, with fish and other creatures swimming by. To my left, I saw a boy sitting on the edge of the dock with a guitar.

He was dressed in faded blue overalls that barely hid his chunky frame. He leaned against one of the dock pillars as his shoeless feet dangled over the water. He was older than me, maybe in his twenties.

His guitar was old but looked as if it was well-loved. The surface was chipped as the beautiful oak color faded in certain parts, giving it a weathered appeal. Oh, the stories I'm sure this guitar could tell.

The boy held his head down, focusing on nothing but his guitar. His fingers massaged the strings, sending beautiful notes floating towards Heaven itself. Every note was deliberate and intentional. He began to sing:

> "I'd pray for you more than me,
> I'd cross the oceans and swim the seas,
> I'd trade all the money and the gold
> To live out our story never told
> To touch your cheek, that's never kissed
> For you will always be my only wish."

As his words floated into the gentle sunset, his emotions poured out from his heart. A fly landed on his guitar and he slowly lifted his hand as to not scare the insect. Seconds later, he watched as the fly soared away, and he let out an audible sigh.

His fingers found their place back on the strings. When he looked up, he finally noticed I was there. He seemed as if he was caught doing something illegal.

"I'm sorry. I'll stop," the boy said apologetically.

"No, don't. It's beautiful. Who is she?"

"Who?" he replied, and I gave him a knowing smile.

He held his head down, staring back at his guitar. His fingers fidgeted against the strings.

"Susan. Her na…na…name is Susan." He continued to look down, clearly embarrassed by his stutter.

"She's the most beaut…beautiful girl I've ever," he stuttered and eventually finished with "seen. I can't really talk that well. But whenever I sing, I fee…fee…feel…"

"Brave," I said as if I knew exactly what he was going through.

"Yes, ma'am. Brave."

"Does she know? That you like her?"

He let out a slight smile. "No, ma'am." His head dropped once more. "I can't. I've tried, but the words d…don't come out right, ya know?"

My mind goes back to Greg and I wondered if these thoughts crossed his mind before he kissed me. The thought filled my heart with warmth. I honestly didn't know what to feel at that moment.

"How do you know it's love? I mean, how do you know it's real?"

"Ma'am, it's like…you know when you're sick and can't br…bre…breathe very well?"

"Yeah."

"Well, it's like that first day after you get bet…better and can finally take that deep bre…bre…" Frustration rose from his face. He exhaled slowly. "Breath, without fear of being in pain. It's…"

"Freeing?" I interrupted.

"Yes, ma'am. Freeing." He gave me another smile. "Very freeing, ma'am." And then, he was gone.

Chapter 30

Weeks had passed and it seemed like my close-knit friends were growing apart. Autumn slowly separated from the group. The constant run-ins with Kim were becoming too much for her. Our friendship dwindled even though we still greeted each other and sent the occasional text back and forth. Even her podcast, Autumn's World, took a more political vibe, highlighting the racial inequalities that plagued our local community. Her fan base had doubled and she finally felt she was making a real difference. I was happy for her.

Kim wasn't much different. We didn't grow apart the same way, but I sensed that she felt nervous around me; like she was constantly walking on eggshells. Sometimes, I would catch her leg twitching. She would often do that when a big test was coming up or if a guy she liked asked her out.

I felt weird asking her about it. I guess I could understand the bizarre treatment. How can you act normal around someone after they had lost someone they loved? Heck, maybe I was the one being closed off.

The only true rock in my life besides my dad was Greg. He was always there whenever I needed to talk and he never failed to put a smile on my face. I enjoyed listening to him tell me stories about his brothers and the trouble they got into. It always made me feel normal. I knew it was weird, but it was comforting and at the time, I could use all the comfort I could get. No matter what bad things life handed me, life would always go on.

That Sunday, after working with CB and Mr. Greene, Kim asked me to hang out to talk. Minus taking the bus to and from school, we hadn't really hung out by ourselves since Dre's death. Plus, I figured this would be my chance to see what was on her mind and why she was so off around me.

We met at the convenience store, and we shared a Slurpee; a great way to drown our sorrows.

"So, what do you think?" she asked as she grabbed the drink from my hand.

"About what?" I replied.

"The trial. Do you think…I mean, how do you think it's going to go?"

She took her sip and passed it back to me. I took a small sip and used that time to try to figure out an answer. "Rough. Very very rough," I emphasized every word.

"Yeah, I thought so. Listen, I have to talk to you. There's something you should know." She put the drink down and turned to face me. *Uh oh, this was never a good way for a conversation to start.* Still, I looked forward to her being open with me.

Of course, last time she said, "There's something you should know," we were in the second grade, and she told me that her family was moving. Luckily, it was only down the street, but when you're seven and your best friend says they are moving, the world seems like it is officially ending.

Our eyes were locked as she placed her hand on mine.

"Well, look guys. It's the killer's little sister."

I looked up to find good old skin-headed Erik hopping out of a familiar jeep. Two of his friends quickly joined, snickering in the background. I jumped up instantly, inadvertently kicking over our Slurpee. I clenched my fist. I was about to knock a racist little punk out.

As I lunged forward, Kim grabbed my arm, making my fists narrowly miss the tip of his nose. He stepped back, surprised by my reaction but quickly tried to play it off as if he meant to flinch.

"Someone should put you in your place," Erik threatened.

"I wish the cops would do their jobs and lock all these animals up," one of his friends said.

"Yeah. It'd be a lot safer for us respectable citizens," the other added.

My vision was locked on Erik and everything else was a blur. All I saw was red. My heart was pounding in my chest, and my breathing was getting shallower. I was ready for war.

"Why don't you just get out of here?" Kim yelled, making a shoeing gesture with her hands.

"Why don't you make us?"

"Yeah," the other friend echoed, taunting immaturely. Erik reached in his pocket and slid out a butterfly knife. He gripped the unopened knife as his eyes scanned mine. I narrowed my eyes, still reaching forward.

"Y'all get from in front of my store. Quit causing trouble," Mrs. Kumar yelled, peeking her head out of the store's front door. She held a broom and made a sweeping motion for us to leave.

"Let's get out of here, guys. I'm bored anyway." Erik stared at me one last time and spat a black substance on the sidewalk next to me. "I'll be seeing you, little girl." He slid the knife into his pocket and hopped back into the jeep.

I was shaking with anger. All I wanted to do was hit Erik with something, anything. I was furious. As I shook like a California earthquake, I felt soft hands against my cheeks and Kim had slowly entered my field of vision. She pressed her forehead against mine and whispered, "Breathe!"

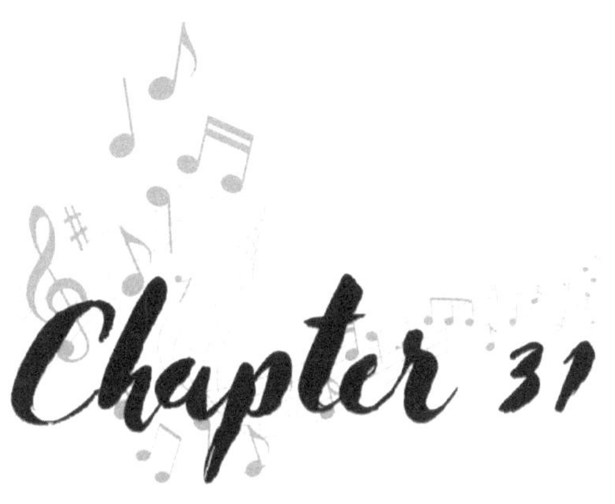

Chapter 31

"But Dad, this isn't fair." I leaned back on the couch, folding my arms.

"Miracle, we think it's best if you didn't go."

"But aren't I, like, the star witness or something? What did CB and Mr. Greene say?"

"We spoke to them, and they think it's the right decision." My dad's voice stayed calm.

"But…" I shook my head and bit my bottom lip. "I need to be there."

My dad's hand made its way to my knee. "No, Bubble Gum, you don't."

I lowered my head.

"This trial will be the second toughest thing you'll have to experience." I didn't have to wonder about the first. I knew. "CB, Mr. Greene and I…uh…and your mother want you to only go to the courtroom when you have to. Plus, CB says the first few days of the trial will be about what they can and can't say during the trial. You won't be missing anything."

Our eyes met. My arms slowly unfolded, and I nodded.

"Okay." I took a deep breath. "Okay."

"Thank you, Bubble Gum." He pressed me into him and hugged me. I returned the hug.

That night, my thoughts raced around my head, and I realized there was no way I was getting any sleep. I decided to do something I rarely ever did, check my social media account to see what the rest of the world was up to. My pointer finger slid through the many booty-shaking videos and the hilarious cat falling off the couch videos until I saw a podcast by Autumn and my heart stopped.

There he was. My brother Dre was posted on her page. The title read "A Fallen Angel," and it had over two-thousand likes. My nerves were a mess, but my finger slowly slid to the play button and I watched, not knowing what was to come.

The video began.

"What's up, Fam. It's your girl, Autumn Willow. I'm here with Dre Jenkins."

"Hey, everyone." Dre tilted his head to the side, flashing a huge smile at the camera.

"So, as you know, Fam, this series is all about interviewing the people, so let's begin."

Dre nodded.

"Dre, what are your plans for the future? What do you want to do after high school?"

He put his hand on his chin and rubbed his wannabe goatee. "Honestly, I haven't really spent much time thinking about it. I know college for sure, but I still haven't found my purpose after high school, ya know? Probably something with kids."

"Kids?" Autumn questioned.

Kids? Maybe I didn't know my brother as well as I thought. I never knew that.

"Yeah, I mean, recently, I've been thinking about becoming a teacher or coach or something."

"What made you have that thought?"

"Honestly?" he paused. "My little sister."

My eyes started to tear up. *Me? Why me?*

"My little sister is the most amazing person I've ever met, and ya know, as her big brother, it's my job to look after her. But sometimes, I feel like she's my big sister. I try to teach her how dumb guys can be and to be street smart, but she teaches me how to be a better dude."

"Miracle's cool like that," Autumn added.

The waterworks were on full blast by this time and my face was drenched in tears.

"What exactly does she teach you?"

"How to love and how I deserve to be loved, ya know? Don't get me wrong, I'm no punk or anything. But she has a unique way of making people feel special, to inspire people to aim for greatness. That's what I want to give to others, especially kids. It's hard surviving in these streets."

The video cut off. I sat there, staring at my phone, at the freeze-frame image of Dre's smile displayed on the screen. I couldn't look away. I couldn't turn it off. *My hero.*

Chapter 32

I laid in my bed that night, wide awake. My senses were heightened as everything seemed magnified. The deafening sound of the air conditioner roared like giants as streetlights streamed through the blinds like spotlights.

I'll never get any sleep at this rate, I thought.

Frustrated, I got out of bed and crept down the hall, trying not to disturb the rest of the family. As my bare feet pressed against the cool kitchen tile, I was caught off guard to see my father awake. He was deep in a trance, eyes staring at the wall while his mind wandered elsewhere.

He hummed a song, a familiar tune he'd hummed when things were on his mind. I had asked him about it when I was younger, but he basically played it off and said it was from his military days. I assumed it was something he learned in the Air Force and I thought nothing else of it.

He must have sensed my presence and finally looked up as the humming continued. Once our eyes met, the world suddenly went dark.

The familiar cold chill spread across my body as darkness covered me and the humming was the only sound in this otherwise still void. The sweet melody danced in the air like a dove. Then, my chest squeezed as my breathing became labored. The moist air clung to my lungs as sweat poured onto my body.

I opened my eyes to find myself lying in tall grass. Fog rested over the surrounding area and visibility was low. Still, I could feel the nibbling of small insects all over my body.

I was in a jungle or forest or something. It reminded me of all those old Rambo movies. My pajamas were transformed into a camouflaged outfit and I held a black rifle. My back ached as a heavy backpack rested on my shoulders, limiting my mobility.

I was about to stand up to get my bearings when I heard it. The same melody my dad always hummed. I searched through the fog to find another man, dressed in the same outfit, carrying the same rifle lying close by, maybe ten yards away.

He softly sang my dad's song.

"Take my breath away.
Take my soul today.
Take me as I am.
Take me or be damned.

I sit alone tonight.

Wondering will I fight.

Take my breath away.

Take my soul tonight."

A hand shot out from the grass and the forest went silent. The hand belonged to a man roughly three feet away. He turned back. A stretched nose made up most of his long narrow face, darkened by black makeup. His eyes were sunken.

He turned his head to the front as his eyes zigzagged from left to right, scanning the surroundings, looking for something. Then, he raised his arm, motioning forward. The silent command resulted in six other men emerging from the foggy bottom. All armed. All scanning.

I followed. The bag threw my balance off, but I found my footing on the muddy floor. The group slowly and deliberately advanced. I did the same.

Suddenly, the leading man raised his arm, and the forest went silent, once again. The men dropped down to one knee and readied their guns. I gripped mine tighter even though I had no idea how to use it.

The silence seemed to last forever. I held my breath as I searched the forest, unsure what or who I was looking for. The lead guy raised his hand once again and made a forward motion. The men slowly stood up and began walking, still scanning the area and gripping their weapons tightly.

"Clyde, I can't wait to get out of this hell hole," whispered the man a few steps away from me. He gave me a slight smile and continued. "You know, Big Momma would kill me if I don't make it."

"Levar, zip it," whispered another man a few feet behind us. Levar looked at me, smiled, and placed his finger in front of his mouth, gesturing to be quiet. Even though I knew this wasn't the environment for small talk, I returned the smile.

We continued through the forest, making our way through prickly tree branches and disgusting swampland. The worst was the mosquitoes. They clung to us like magnets on a refrigerator. As we continued, Levar began softly humming my dad's song.

"Sergeant Levar, I thought I told you to zip it. Now zip your…" The man suddenly trailed off and narrowed his eyes. An uncomfortable silence lingered in the air.

A loud explosion erupted in front of the man to my right, shattering the silence. The blast threw my body into the air, slamming me on the damp forest floor. High-pitched ringing pounded against my eardrums and the world began to spin. My vision was blurry…everything was blurry.

I saw hints of bright lights and heard faint murmuring, but I couldn't make out any of the noise. I shook my head and tried to get to my feet, but my knees gave way. I shook my head again, shaking off the cobwebs in my ears. Still ringing.

I raised my head as a giant blur rushed towards me. I was too weak to move, and my vision didn't assist the situation. My hand roamed around the grass, searching for my gun.

Where is it? Where is it?

The giant blur approached, lunging towards me. It was screaming something at me. I was too weak to fight it off. I fought but my arms and legs were wobbly messes. I managed to lean forward, only to be pressed down again. I was pinned. My head pushed down to the ground, mud seeping into my mouth.

"No," I screamed. "Get off me."

The blur yelled, but it was garbled. Soon, the blur began to take shape. Small features started to form as one unrecognizable blur became an eye, then lips followed by a long, black-covered nose.

I stopped fighting. My body went limp as he screamed again. His voice was barely audible, but I could read his lips: "Stay down!"

The forest filled with smoke and debris from the explosions. Flashes of light blasted from our rifles. I knocked the side of my head a few times with my hand to quiet the ringing.

Once my hearing started to return, I heard a mix of screaming and gunshots, followed by an explosion. Then another. A series of loud, intense gunshots flashed through the air.

Then, my eyes fell upon Levar. His body lay motionless. His eyes drained of color. Blood painted his chest like an artist's canvas. There was no more singing. I reached out for him and suddenly, another explosion. My body jerked back, and once again, I slammed into the ground. Darkness.

Chapter 33

"Can't sleep either? Pull up a chair."

My eyes sprung open as I let out an audible gasp. I strained my neck, searching my surroundings. My hand scanned my body, searching for injuries.

"You, okay?" my dad asked.

He pushed out the chair next to him and motioned for me to sit. I looked up and forced myself to relax my body. I tried to act normal, but I had to admit that my mind was still a little shell-shocked from what I saw. It seemed so real.

"Thanks," I said, making myself comfortable. Dad slid over the plate, which had a half-eaten slice of German chocolate cake.

I slid my finger across the plate, scooping up the frosting.

"Let me get you a fork," he said with a smile. He proceeded to the kitchen and cut me a slice. He knew me too well.

"You know the song you always hum?" I asked. I didn't know where that question came from, but it blurted out of me like an uncontrollable sneeze.

"Yep," he replied, grabbing a fork from the drawer.

"Who taught it to you?" He paused and took a deep breath.

Oh crap. I just opened pandora's box.

"It was…" he paused and then continued making his way to the table. "A good buddy from the military used to sing it."

"Oh." I didn't know if I should keep pressing. "What was his name?"

His eyes met mine, and then he looked back at his cake and fidgeted with his fork.

"You know what? Never mind, Dad. I shouldn't have…." I tried to backtrack, but it was too late.

"Levar. Sergeant David Levar."

Holy crap. My mind went crazy with questions. Was my vision real? It was so vivid and the explosions…I could still hear the ringing. There was no way. Levar… Oh, Levar. If it was real, it meant my dad had lived it. He had watched his friend die.

"He was a great guy. Funny." He continued without me asking him to. I just stared. "Originally from Austin, Texas."

"Austin? Have you ever been there?"

He frowned. "Just once." I could see my dad's eyes starting to tear up. I'd never seen him cry. Well, once, when I was younger, he accidentally hit a dog with his car. I was about five years old. We both balled as we sat next to the dog in the street. Even after the dog waddled away, we still sat there crying. It was pretty funny afterward but definitely not at the time.

I slid my hand on top of his. "We don't have to talk about it. I'm sorry I asked, Daddie-O."

"You know I never talked to you about my military life. Heck, I never talked to your mom, either."

He stared at his hands as if he was waiting for them to reveal what to say next.

"Take my breath away…take my soul today." He wiped a tear away and bit his lower lip. Then sighed. "Levar was a good guy. He got me through a lot of dark times." He sighed again but continued.

"I was deployed to this one unit. He had been there a few months before me, so he took me under his wing and made sure I was taken care of. Really…really good guy." He shook his head, remembering his dear friend.

"Did he die? You said he *was* a good guy," I stumbled, not knowing the correct way to ask.

"We were on a recon patrol and got ambushed. Half our men were injured, legs were blown off, arms ripped to shreds and…" He stopped. I think he finally realized he was going into too much graphic detail for his young daughter. But I didn't mind. I wanted to know what dark secrets kept this quiet man in the shadows.

Suddenly, I remembered the nights waking up to my mom screaming, "It's over." I thought they were fighting at the time, but now it makes more sense.

They weren't fighting. He was having flashbacks and reliving the horrors of war. Now I understood, it was the war she was yelling about. The war was over, but I guessed for him, it seemed like the war never ended.

I squeezed his hand to let him know he could continue, and he did.

"Levar was one of four who didn't make it. I remember his eyes when he died. They stayed open. It's those eyes that keep me up at night. Not the screams, the gunshots, the explosions, but the eyes." And then it happened. My father, who I adored more than anything, finally let all the feelings he had bottled up flow freely, and he cried. And then I cried.

Chapter 34

I'm not sure how long we stayed at the table, but my mom was waking both of us before I knew it. The area next to me was wet and I wasn't sure if it was from my tears or just drool. But knowing me, it was likely a mixture of both.

While my parents got dressed, I fixed them a hearty breakfast of two eggs, microwaved sausage and buttered toast. Nothing was burnt, so I figured the cooking class was paying off, especially without Greg next to me. I placed their plates on the dinner table and poured two large glasses of orange juice. I wanted them to be fueled for the trial. They appreciated the gesture.

After they left, I turned on the TV and flipped through the channels. Various news agencies were covering the trial and I watched on the edge of my seat. I reached on the side table, grabbed my phone, and sent a text message.

Twenty minutes passed and there was a knock on the door. I opened the door to find a friendly face.

"What's up, lady?"

"Hey, Greg, come on in." He shot me a smile and ducked inside.

"Thanks." I could hear the hesitation in his voice, but I had already explained my parents were in court. I grabbed a soda for him and handed him a bag of chips.

"Thanks." He sat down, making himself comfortable.

We watched as my parents arrived at the courthouse. CB walked alongside them, like a bodyguard protecting her clients. Reporters bombarded their arrival, hurling questions left and right.

"Do you think your son was innocent?"

"Are you doing this for the money?"

"Do you think cops can't be trusted?"

"Leave them alone," I shouted at the screen. Greg sat silently. Cameras returned to the news reporters as they spoke to the television audience.

"You sad you're not there?"

"Not really. I mean, yeah, but no." I turned to him.

"Yeah, I get it."

Suddenly, my jaw dropped and time stood still. Greg turned to the TV and instantly realized why I sat paralyzed.

"And Jacob Zander just arrived with his parents," a news reporter announced.

"Jacob, why were you silent about the incident?" one reporter asked.

"Mr. Zander, how is your son dealing with this tragedy?" asked another.

"But I thought he was…" I stuttered.

"Yeah, me too."

The news reporter leaned forward and pressed her finger to her ear. "Meghan," the voice of a broadcaster started, "why has Jacob Zander been so silent before trial? Did his family or lawyer speak on that?"

"Yes, Jerry. According to the family's lawyer, they were assigned to witness protection following the incident," said Meghan Clooney.

"I thought he was dead," I repeated. I stared into the TV, absorbing every word being said.

"Witness protection? I thought that was something they made up in the movies," Greg acknowledged.

"I thought he was dead," I repeated again, slowly. My eyes weld up. Greg placed his hand on my back. My expression soon changed.

"Are you smiling?"

I turned to Greg and placed my hands on his legs, which startled him, and he jumped up a little. "Get it?" I leaned into him.

"Get what?" Greg asked, confused.

"My brother isn't a killer!"

Greg dropped his shoulders. "Oh yeah."

I stared into his eyes. His eyes moved to my lips and then flashed down towards the ground. My hands moved to his cheeks and I pulled him into me.

Our lips met once again. Greg's lips were soft and his cheek was smooth like silk as it rubbed against mine. My eyes closed as the moment swept over me. The weightless feeling floated over me as my heart landed on clouds. *Now, this is how a kiss should be.*

Our lips pulled apart and I tried to stare into his eyes, but they were still closed.

"Damn," he muttered.

Chapter 35

The next few hours were spent watching every minute of the trial. My right hand rested on Greg's left as he used his other hand to devour our chips.

The courtroom was crowded. People were squeezed into the seats while others stood along the sides and back of the room.

"I didn't realize there would be so many people."

"Yeah," Greg said with concern in his voice.

The sheer number of people sent shivers down my spine.

The trial began when Judge Alexander Rodriguez arrived. He was a Hispanic male in his seventies who, according to the news, had been practicing law for over forty years. He was well respected and known for his ability to snuff out BS in the courtroom. I liked him.

The first twenty minutes of the trial was filled with Judge Rodriguez laying down the rules for his courtroom.

"A life was lost. Let's make sure we honor the dead by respecting one another and these four walls. Understood?" Judge Rodriguez began. And with that, opening statements started.

Mr. Greene went first. My expectations of him were well founded. He communicated the "outrageous travesty" that took place and his desire to prove that, without a shadow of a doubt, the death of my brother was unlawful, inexcusable, and downright murder. The jurors seemed to take an interest in his opening statement. Some jurors showed no emotion whatsoever, while others nodded in agreement.

"Thank you for participating in this process and I urge you to bear in mind that this is a legal proceeding to find the truth. Moreover, my team will bring you the truth during the entirety of this trial. Thank you." Mr. Greene walked back to his table. I could see my parents behind him, arm in arm, with CB sitting next to them.

Then the other lawyer stood up and adjusted his black suit, Jonathan Chivers. Mr. Chivers was likely in his late forties and his once black hair was replaced with greyish white. He had a finely-shaped mustache that ran its way to his low-cut beard. The lawyer was slim, tall, and reeked of confidence. He placed his rounded glasses on and headed towards the jury.

"Good morning, ladies and gentlemen of the jury. On 8 October 2021, two Lancaster City Police Officers, Derek Wright, and Keith Gladwell shot and killed Andre King Jenkins as he held a 9mm pistol. The shoot was in adherence to police protocol. By presenting sound evidence and witness testimony, I will prove that both officers were justified and are not guilty of any wrongdoing. Thank you for your participation." With that, he turned and walked back to his seat. Brief and to the point.

"Your honor, I'd like to call Officer Gladwell to the stand, please," Mr. Greene said.

Buzzcut!

The crowd made a few side comments as the officer stood up, adjusted his suit, and proceeded to the witness stand. He didn't seem nervous or anything, just totally unemotional. It was as if he had been through this process multiple times and was a trained expert.

"Booooo!" Greg shouted. I smiled.

The bailiff walked in front of him and made him say and spell his full name.

"Officer Keith Gladwell, no middle name. K E I T H G L A D W E L L."

"Would you like to affirm or swear on the holy book?" the bailiff asked.

"Affirm," he responded. *Of course, he doesn't believe in God,* I thought. After affirming to tell the truth, he was ordered to sit down and the questioning began.

Chapter 36

"Let's go, Mr. G. You got this!"

"Yeah, he does," Greg agreed.

Mr. Greene checked his notes one last time and proceeded to the center of the room.

"Good morning, Mr. Gladwell. Please tell the court what is your profession."

"I'm a patrol officer in the Lancaster Police Department," he responded.

"And how long have you been working as a patrol officer in the Lancaster PD?"

"Sixteen years," he said. His answer seemed smug to me as if Mr. Greene was wasting his time.

Mr. Greene continued asking about Officer Gladwell's experience as a police officer. They covered his previous training, which led to his current position and his various locations of employment. There were also questions about his certification process. It seemed he was still up to date on all his qualifications. And then, Mr. Greene started asking about his interaction with Dre and me.

"Why did you stop Andre Jenkins?"

"I received a 10-107," he paused and waited for Mr. Greene to ask to clarify what a 10-107 was.

"10-107 meaning a suspicious person, just to clarify for the jurors," Mr. Greene said, motioning to the jury.

"Yes, a suspicious person."

"What was the description of said suspicious person?"

"African American male, between the ages of fourteen and twenty-one, wearing blue jeans and a white t-shirt, accompanied by a female, African American, in the same age range," he responded.

"That's, like, our entire city," I muttered.

"Yep," Greg agreed.

"And what was this suspicious person allegedly doing?"

"Public disturbance," he said.

"Please, go on."

"We saw two people who fit the description, so we called it in and proceeded to question them. Once we pulled up, we could tell the male was agitated. We tried to defuse the situation by engaging in peaceful conversation, but at this time, there was no consoling him."

Raged engulfed me. I tensed up, ready to lash out at the TV. Greg squeezed my hand harder. I shook my head in acknowledgment and took several deliberate breaths.

"Breathe, it'll be okay." He always had a way of calming me down, my light during the darkest times.

Officer Gladwell continued, "When we got out of the car, we questioned them about where they were going."

"And what did they say?" Mr. Greene asked.

"To study. Miracle Jenkins told me and Officer Wright she was studying with her friend, Ms. Kimberly Blair."

Mr. Greene nodded. "What happened next, Officer Gladwell?"

"Without any further reason to detain them, we let them go. We told them to carry on about their days. So, the two began to walk up the steps to their friend's house."

"Okay. Please continue."

"We were about to head back to the car when my partner alerted me to a gun."

"You didn't see it first?"

"No, he alerted me by shouting 'gun.' When I turned around, Andre had the weapon, raising it to a firing position. All I saw was the barrel of the gun staring down at me."

"What did he do before he raised the gun?"

"I didn't see. Like I said, he was going up the stairs."

"Why do you think he went from going up the stairs, leading to his freedom, to pointing a gun at you and your partner, which resulted in his death?"

"I can't speak to the mindset of a criminal, Sir."

"Criminal, what crime did he commit?"

Officer Gladwell paused and looked at his lawyer. "Well, he did point a gun at me and my partner, so there's that." Low murmurs were heard throughout the courtroom.

"Thank you for your time." Mr. Greene turned to head back to his table. Before he sat down, he turned back to the witness stand.

"Actually, one last question. How many shots did you fire?"

Officer Gladwell paused again to look at his lawyer.

"Do you need me to repeat the question?"

He looked at Mr. Greene. His eyes looked like death rays, pointing right at the lawyer. "Fifteen."

The crowd erupted.

"Murderer," one person shouted.

The pounding of the gavel echoed in the court as Judge Rodriguez tried to gain control of his precious courtroom.

Moments later, the defendant's attorney walked up to the witness stand, greeted Officer Gladwell, and thanked him for his service. Officer Gladwell remained composed throughout the questioning, minus that one slip up. Hopefully, the jury didn't believe his version of the story. He had just made it seem like Dre was hunting officers, which wasn't true. Not true at all.

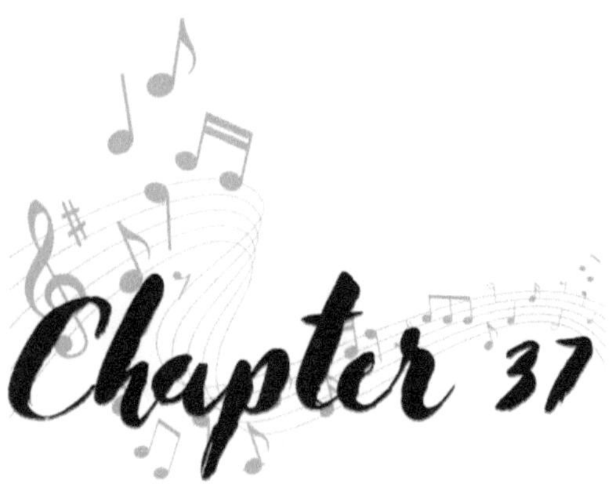

Chapter 37

Click.

"What are you doing?" Greg questioned.

"I can't watch anymore. It's driving me crazy not being there. I should be there." I threw my hands in the air in protest.

"Sorry. Well, what do you want to do?"

"Run."

"Wait, what? I was kind of hoping you'd say make out." He shrugged his shoulders. My head shot in his direction as my eyes narrowed. "Or not." He smiled. *Oh, that smile. Gets me every time.* Greg was usually a very timid person. It was rare for him to be so bold. I guess my lips could change a man. Good to know...

After a few minutes of kissing, I kicked Greg out so I could get ready. I needed to clear my mind, and I couldn't do that with him around.

Thirty minutes later, I was already over a mile into my run. The 7-Eleven and a collection of local motels were already behind me. My earbuds rested snugly in my ears as my black Nike t-shirt and shorts combo clung to my body. Kanye West blared in my ears and my feet pounded against the pavement upon every beat of the song.

I felt free. There were no reporters to avoid, no lawyers asking me questions, nothing; just a girl and her music. Even my breathing was on point, two inhales followed by two exhales. My head was up and my hips were forward. My arms swung close to my body. I was in my flow.

On the corner of West Avenue J, I made a right, passing my favorite Chinese restaurant. We ordered from there at least once a week. I always got the General Tso's chicken with white rice. *"Maybe that can be my post-run meal,"* I thought, huffing my way past the enticing aroma.

Moments later, an eerie feeling of being watched rushed over me. I looked over my shoulder to find a police car behind me, creeping forward. Its speed matched mine. I pushed on and extended my stride.

The car sped to match my acceleration. I knew I wasn't going to outrun it, so I stopped. It shadowed my movement. I turned around to see two officers staring at me. Mischievous smiles decorated their faces as they shared a few laughs.

Suddenly, the car crept forward. When it was alongside me, the window slowly rolled down. The Black officer in the passenger seat reached out his arm and rested it out the window, tapping his gaudy class ring against the car door. The clinging was annoying.

His partner, a white male in his late thirties, spoke on a cell phone but never lost eye contact with me. The use of a cell phone made me question the legality of this encounter.

I wanted to move. My warm legs were stiffening, but I feared any sudden movement would set off alarms in their heads. The song Hip Hop is Dead blasted in my ears. I closed my eyes as my head danced to the beat. Then, I turned and ran.

My feet pounded on the ground as my legs shot up. My arms sliced through the air while I dug deeper and pushed harder. I lost control of my breathing as I pressed forward.

Push, I told myself.

Push!

Push!

I rounded the corner onto Sierra Highway. My body soon shut down, unable to keep that Olympic pace. My sprint turned to a moderate jog until, eventually, I started to walk. My hands found solace on my hips as I tilted my head back. The dry desert air was refreshing. I turned to find my stalkers stopped at the corner. They continued to stare. I shot them a smile and then turned around and went home.

Chapter 38

Day two of the trial had arrived and my nerves were restless. After a quick breakfast, my parents and I readied ourselves and headed to the courthouse.

The Michael Antonovich Antelope Valley Courthouse looked futuristic, with a large half-circle covered in glass. The half-dome squished between two long rectangular buildings, while tall palm trees were positioned along the main walking path.

This is where reporters stood waiting for our arrival, cameras and microphones in hand, on the ready. Protesters gathered cutting off a section of the parking lot in the front of the building. Their signs waved high as their shouts for justice and equality reverberated off the glass building.

We didn't even make it to the first step before we were bombarded by reporters.

"Did your son try to shoot the cops?" a reporter shouted, sticking her microphone in our faces.

"Which gang is your son affiliated with?" said another.

"Did the first day of trial go as expected?" added another.

"Put your heads down and just walk," a familiar voice said. I looked up, and there was Mr. Greene with his arm extended out to us.

"Head down!" he commanded. He quickly ushered us through the swarm of reporters until we reached the glass doors. As soon as the doors closed, the sound of the reporters was drowned out.

"Sorry about that. Are you guys okay?"

My parents assured him we were, and I nodded.

Mr. Greene led us through security and down the main hall. I had never been in a courthouse before. It was a lot larger than I expected. Across from the main doors were stairs that led up several flights. Offices and courtrooms shouldered each other along both sides of the building. It was definitely not like the television shows.

It was intimidating just being in there, but the overwhelming feeling I had when we entered the building was nothing compared to my feelings once we arrived at the courtroom.

"This is where the trial will be taking place. We'll be sitting in the front alongside CB and behind Mr. Greene, okay?" my dad explained, I gave him a nod. The security guard stationed in front of the courtroom opened the door and my entourage piled in. I took a deep breath and followed.

As soon as we entered, all heads turned to us as soft murmurs from the crowd quickly filled the room. If this wasn't awkward before, it was definitely awkward now. I scanned the room and saw a lot of people, most of whom I didn't recognize.

Rieko sat on the left; his eyes locked on mine. My mind flashed back to Detective Berry asking about Dre's gang affiliation because of Rieko. He raised his fist up and shot me a smile. I nodded. Autumn was posted in the back wearing a black t-shirt that read NJNP! A few more of Dre's friends were scattered in the crowd.

My eyes continued to scan the room. I finally saw two more familiar faces through the sea of strangers; Kim and Greg. They were sitting right next to our reserved spots. Their presence warmed my heart.

Greg and Kim scooted over to give us room when we got to our aisle. Kim greeted me with a hug, and Greg did the same. I won't lie; I may have held onto Greg's hug a little longer than Kim's. Hopefully, no one noticed.

"Thanks for coming, guys," I said while getting settled in.

"Of course," Greg replied.

"You know we got you," Kim added.

"This seems way more intense than on TV. This is crazy," Greg said, peering over the crowded courtroom.

"I figured it would be. I just hope everything goes smoothly."

Kim leaned over Greg and took my hand. "Are you ready?"

I shook my head in response. How could anyone be ready for something like this? I would have to relive the most tragic day of my life in front of a courtroom of strangers who saw my brother as nothing but a criminal.

"All rise for the honorable Judge Rodriguez," the bailiff announced, bringing the crowd to silence.

Before I knew it, we had started.

Chapter 39

"Ms. Miracle Jenkins to the stand, please," requested Mr. Chivers. I let out a deep breath and stood to my feet. All eyes were honed on me as I made my way to the witness stand. Every step was filled with more nervousness and dread, but as I passed CB, she shot me a wink and a nod to reassure me. I returned her nod.

As a million thoughts swam in my head, I stood facing the lawyer and the rest of the world.

"Please state and spell your name," the bailiff commanded.

"Miracle Lorene Jenkins. M I R A C L E L O R E N E J E N K I N S." My hand trembled as it lay across the bible.

I shifted my body around in the seat as the lawyer approached.

"Did your brother have any encounters with Erik Oliver or Jacob Zander before this incident?"

"Yes."

The lawyer stood there, waiting patiently. He raised his eyebrows and said, "Please elaborate."

"Erik lives in Kim's neighborhood. One day he and Jake…I mean, Jacob, were trying to get in a fight with my brother and our friends."

"Interesting. What started the fight?"

"I don't know."

"I'm sorry, can you please elaborate? What do you mean you don't know? I mean, you were there, correct?"

At this point, the lawyer leaned against the witness stand, tapping his wedding ring against the wood.

"I wasn't there when it started. I came in the middle of it."

"Oh, okay, so then you can't say for sure who was actually starting the fight, correct?"

"Well…I…" my thoughts were jumbled, and I tried not to stutter. "Yeah, I guess. But…"

"I see." The lawyer paused. He walked back to his table, shuffling through some documents. "Please explain what happened when you saw Erik and Jacob on 8 October." He looked up from the table, waiting for my response.

The dryness of my mouth felt like desert sand.

"They had thrown a burrito at us while we were walking to Kim's house."

Laughter began in the audience. The judge cleared his throat to get everyone's attention, and Mr. Chivers continued.

"A burrito? Oh my. And then what happened?"

My eyes went from the lawyer directly to my shoes. I closed my eyes and took in a few deep breaths. Tears started to form on the edges of my eyes, but I wouldn't allow them to fall. Not right now. I had to be strong.

"Is this when your brother pulled a gun at Mr. Oliver?"

My head slowly began to rise.

"Yes," I said softly.

"Did you know your brother had a gun?"

"No."

"Throughout the trial, Mr. Greene has brought witnesses to speak about your brother's character, labeling him as a respectful, loyal, kind young man. Would you agree with that characterization?"

"Of course, my brother was…"

"Then please explain what a kind young man such as your brother would be doing carrying a gun."

I paused. I looked back down. "I don't know why he had a gun."

"Was he threatened by anyone? Maybe that's why he had a gun?" Mr. Chivers crept closer to the witness stand. "Or maybe he wanted to hurt someone. What do you think?"

"He wouldn't hurt anyone."

"Are you saying he needed protection, then, Ms. Jenkins?"

"Maybe."

"From whom?"

"I don't know."

"Erik, maybe?" he paused. "Do you know why he was aiming it at the officers, then?"

"No... I mean, he wasn't. He slipped."

"So, he slipped, grabbed a gun, and aimed it at the officers?"

My heart was pounding, and I couldn't help but curl my hands into a fist.

"Did your brother have a vendetta against the police?"

"What? No."

"So, he liked the police then?" Mr. Chivers asked.

"No, no one does."

Cheers could be heard from the audience. Mr. Chivers waited until the crowd died down and continued, "I do."

"Well, you don't live where we live."

"If I did, do you think I'd hate the police?"

"Probably."

"Enough to shoot one?"

I paused, falling right into his trap. He tricked me. He tricked me into saying the one thing I promised never to say…that there was a chance my brother was guilty.

"No further questions, your honor, but I would like the privilege of cross-examining at another time, if I may."

"Understood," the judge said. "Mr. Greene, you may cross." Mr. Greene stood up and adjusted his suit. He looked at me, not in disgust like the other lawyer, but with empathy, and then he smiled. His smile put me at ease.

"Ms. Jenkins," he paused. "Miracle, did your brother say anything before he shot the gun?"

I thought for a second. My eyebrows perked up and I spoke. "He said he feared for my life and his."

The court erupted in whispers. Judge Rodriguez cleared his throat once more to settle the crowd.

"Hmm. That doesn't sound like a cold-blooded killer." He paused and stepped closer. "Do you feel safe around the police?"

His question threw me off. I didn't know where he was going or what he wanted me to say. He noticed my hesitation and said, "You can be honest."

I nodded. "No, I don't."

"Why not?"

"My only interaction with them has been negative. The cops stare at me as I cross the street or watch me if we happen to be in the same store together. I seem to always fit the description. I never hear about them rescuing someone or treating people nicely. Don't get me wrong, I know there *are* good police officers out there. But I just don't think they protect and serve in our neighborhood."

Soft murmurs were heard from the crowd.

"Do you think Andre felt the same way?"

Mr. Chivers shot out of his seat. "Objection, she can't speak for her brother, your honor, or know his mindset."

"Your honor, as close as they were, surely, he must have told his little sister how he felt."

Judge Rodriguez rubbed his chin and nodded. "I'll allow it, but tread lightly, Mr. Greene."

"Thank you, your honor." He turned back to face me. "Did your brother ever express his feelings about the police, Miracle?"

"Yes, a few times."

"What did he feel?"

"I object, your honor," Mr. Chivers screamed again. "Whatever she says is…"

"I'll rephrase," Mr. Greene interrupted. "Did he ever express wanting to kill a police officer?"

"No, he wasn't like that."

"Tell us, then, what was he like?" He slowly backed up, giving the floor to me.

"He was sweet. Yeah, he had a tough exterior. But deep down, he was genuine and loyal." My eyes began to tear up. "He looked after me. The only time he ever got in a fight was when he was sticking up for other people. He protected them so they wouldn't get hurt. He was the voice for those who couldn't speak up for themselves."

"He sounds like an amazing big brother."

I wiped my tears away and shook my head. "He was."

"Miracle, I want to ask you to do something very difficult, but it needs to happen."

"Yes, sir."

"Tell me what happened the day of your brother's death."

I closed my eyes and focused on my breathing.

"Yes, sir." I took a sip from the water bottle and began telling the story.

Chapter 40

"They killed him. They killed my big brother." I leaned against the witness stand, my head resting over my arms as I began to sob uncontrollably.

The court erupted in commotion. A man in the back wearing a BLM shirt stood up, shouting, "No justice, no peace!" echoed by several other members in the crowd. This sparked the police officers, who sat behind Officer Gladwell, to stand and protect the officers on trial from the crowd.

The judge pounded his gavel, but it was pointless. It was too late. The bailiff and several other court security guards tried to wrangle people back in their seats, but the craziness ensued.

I looked at my dad. He wrapped his arms around my mom, sheltering her from the madness. Then, he was suddenly pushed from behind, sending his head crashing into the seat in front of him. I jumped up, but the bailiff held me back.

More pounding by the judge.

"Bailiffs, clear this courtroom NOW!"

It took twenty-eight minutes before the last person was herded out of the courtroom. CB led my family to another adjacent room, out of harm's way. We were finally able to catch our breaths.

Once we realized we were safe, my dad gave me a hug and kissed my forehead. I crawled into his chest and the waterworks began once more. My mom sat in the chair along the wall, rocking back and forth.

CB walked over to the mini-refrigerator in the opposite corner. "Help yourself to some water or whatever else you need. I'll be right back." With that, she disappeared into the hallway.

"Did I screw the case up? What if they say he was guilty because I said he didn't like the cops? Can they...?"

"Hush, now. None of that talk." My dad pressed his head on top of mine, serenading me with his familiar tune. I desperately wanted to remain in my dad's arms forever, hoping this feeling of security would last.

The large wooden door slid open, revealing a calm, collected CB. "The judge ordered a recess until the morning. You can go home and get some rest." Then, she walked over and leaned down close to me and whispered, "Thank you for being so brave."

Chapter 41

It took us over an hour to fight through barricades and swarms of people, but we eventually made our way home. My bed was a warm companion as I threw my limp body into its arms.

B_{zzzzzz}.

My phone shook, and I picked it up with the last bit of energy I had left. Six missed calls and twelve text messages. *Those can wait until later,* I thought. My phone fell back on the bed as darkness quickly took over.

The following morning, my legs felt heavy as I moved across the drab carpet. A yawn stretched my face as I rubbed my eyes, trying to remove my cloudy vision. The wall acted as a reliable friend, supporting me as I reached the kitchen.

My parents sat at the table, gripping the handle of their coffee mugs, staring at their reflections in the steaming coffee. Bags lingered under their eyes as their bodies reminded me of statues in central park, beautiful yet void of life.

"Morning," a deeper voice than I was used to slipped from my lips.

"Mr. Greene would like us to come in a little early to prep a cross-examination, Bubble Gum." My dad's pace of speech slowed as if each word took more and more energy. He took a sip. He scrunched up his face as he pushed the mug away. He was never a big coffee drinker.

The two lawyers were waiting for us in the same office we escaped into the previous day. When we walked in, CB and Mr. Greene greeted us with two cups of coffee for my parents and a glass of water for me. I was grateful, but coffee sounded a lot better at this point.

"So, they may ask Miracle to testify again?"

"It's a strong possibility. The judge will afford them that opportunity," Mr. Greene responded.

My father squirmed in his seat while my mom shook her head in disbelief.

"What do you think they'll ask me?"

"Well, given your brother's distrust of the police department and the fact that he did have a gun-"

My mom mumbled something, but it wasn't very clear. It sounded like, "Where did he get a gun," but no one thought to ask her to repeat it. Plus, unfortunately, that fact didn't matter right now. The person who provided him the gun didn't kill my brother. He wasn't our enemy, at least not today.

My eyes found their way to CB, who held her head down. Then, I saw it. A moment of sadness crossed her face. I mean real sadness. It quickly faded and she put her professional mask back on, but for that one moment, I saw it.

People called CB a robot, but maybe this robot was empathetic of our cause. Every case she tried was to protect the rights of another. Every case was because something terrible had happened. No matter who you are or tough you appear to be, it has to eventually take a toll on you. This had to be hard on her, too.

CB cleared her throat and continued. "If I were them, I would ask about his past. Criminal behavior, fights with others and his mental state at the time of the incident."

CB and Mr. Greene spent roughly thirty minutes firing hypothetical questions at me to help me feel more comfortable. My phone kept going off, so eventually, my dad took it away and put it on silent. We all knew this was more important than anything else and I had to have my full attention on Mr. Greene, CB, and the prep work. I couldn't afford to screw this up; not again.

We finished around 9:25 a.m. and had five minutes before the trial started. As we walked into the courtroom, I saw Greg sitting in the same spot as yesterday and Kim standing next to him. Her fingers rapidly punched away on her phone. Greg saw us and stood up. He whispered something to Kim who quickly turned her head to find us approaching. Kim made her way past several folks sitting in the same row. I greeted them with a smile and waved, but the looks on their faces were of terror.

"I've been calling you all night," she said. Her face worried me.

"Yeah, I'm sorry. I've been busy and…"

"They put me on the witness list, Miracle." Her voice crackled. I'd never seen her so shaken up.

"But you didn't see anything. What's the problem?"

"But I…"

"All rise!" The courtroom went silent as the crowd stood to their feet.

I looked nervously at Kim and she did the same. She fidgeted, her leg violently shaking. This wasn't a good sign.

"What's going on?"

"I…" Again, we were interrupted, this time, by my dad. He waved us off as he put his finger to his lips.

After a quick recap of the need for respect and professionalism throughout this hearing process by the judge, round three was underway. I stared at Kim and she placed her trembling hands on mine and squeezed.

"Thank you, your honor. I'd like to call our first witness of the day. Kimberly Ann Blair."

Chapter 42

Mr. Greene sprung from his chair. "Your honor, Ms. Blair is not on the witness list. We need time to vet the witness and…"

"Sir, we just recently found out about her and her testimony. I assure you, your honor, we had no intention of hiding this from Mr. Greene and his team."

"Of course, you did, hence why we are just now finding out about it."

"That's enough gentlemen. I'll allow it just to see what she has to say, but Mr. Chivers, you need to mind your Ps and Qs, because I refuse to have another circus, like yesterday. Do I make myself clear?"

"Absolutely, your honor," the lawyer said.

"Yes, sir," Mr. Greene acknowledged. He sat down and whispered something to CB sitting behind him.

"Ms. Blair, please proceed," ordered the judge.

The world turned to Kim. Our eyes met once more. I stared into the windows of her soul and found fear and dread. She stood up, her hand slipping from mine. Mummers floated in the courtroom.

I swear I could hear her heart pounding in her chest. I reached out to grab her again, but it was too late, she was already making her way to the witness stand. All the nervousness that I had subdued about the trial came rushing back. I didn't know what to expect.

Kim sat on the stand and swore in. The lawyer slithered towards her.

"Ms. Blair, I hope you are well this morning."

She nodded.

"Now, before I begin with my questions, I just want to remind you that you gave an oath before God to tell the truth. Understand?"

"Yes, sir," she stumbled. Her eyes moved back and forth rapidly as if she didn't know what to focus on.

"Good, so let's begin. Is your address 4344A Kirkland Avenue, Lancaster, California?"

"Yes, sir."

"Where were you on 8 October 2021 at approximately 3:45 p.m.?

"In my house."

"How can you be certain?"

"I was waiting at home to hang out with my friend, Miracle."

My dad grabbed my left hand as Greg grabbed my right. My body shook furiously as my breathing quickened.

"Do you need me to repeat the question?"

Kim wiped a trickle of sweat from her brow. "Yes, please."

"Did you see Miracle and Andre outside with Officer Gladwell and Officer Wright?"

She closed her eyes. "Yes, I looked out my window while they were talking to the police officers."

CB looked towards me. I shrugged and mouthed, "I didn't know." CB turned around again, and the courtroom focused on every word Kim uttered.

"Did you see Dre holding the gun?"

Again, she paused.

I thought back to the first day we met; Kindergarten, Ms. Esse's class. She was crying because Freddy Bagwell stole her crayon. I walked over to her table and handed her my blue crayon.

"Ms. Blair?"

And the first time she told me her mom died. We stood over her mom's gravesite for hours, not saying anything. Just holding hands like sisters do.

"Yes. I saw him holding the gun."

The day we sat in horror in a stall in the mall bathroom when I had my first period. My new white shorts were ruined. She slid the change into the machine, causing a small, wrapped, slender object to appear, which we had to Google how to use.

"What was he doing with the gun?"

Her eyes were locked onto mine. My heart raced.

Why didn't she tell me she saw anything? Why didn't she come to me sooner? Why didn't she... Suddenly, all those times she tried to talk to me came rushing back.

"Shit," I said, not realizing I had said it aloud. My dad nudged my arm as the entire room clung to her every word.

The pause ended. "It looked like Dre was aiming it at the officers."

Her last word echoed in the already tense air. My heart stopped. The room began to spin while my vision grew dark. I took one final breath, and then, the world went black.

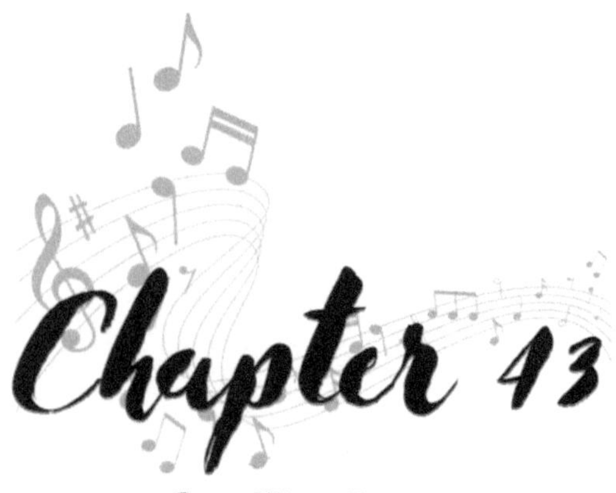

Chapter 43

One Year Later

The packing was almost done. One room remained before a life with divorced parents. I sat with my dad on the cold floor of our garage, sorting boxes of old photo albums and heirlooms. His pile was on the left, and the items that would go to my mom's house on the right.

"Check this out." He handed me a photo of a young girl dressed in pink Minnie Mouse pajamas, arm in arm with an older little boy in a black NWO t-shirt.

"Oh my God. We were so cute."

"You were maybe five then. Dre was trying to teach you to dance to my old records. You'd laugh so hard every time I put them on."

"We were adorable. Ya know, Daddie-O, you made some pretty cute babies."

"Y'all were okay."

He smiled as he ripped open another box. Every now and then, he would freeze at an old item. This had to be hard for him. First, to lose a son, and then, losing the love of his life. He deserved better. We all did.

I grabbed another box from the shelf, blowing off the cobwebs. As the knife sliced open the black masking tape, more photo albums lay stacked on one another. I sighed. This was going to take all day.

I didn't know how to correctly divide photo albums, so I alternated between both parents. One in dad's box, the next one in mom's. How could anyone genuinely divide cherished memories?

As I grabbed another box, the bottom ripped open, sending an album crashing to the floor, which in turn caused several photos to slide across the garage floor.

One item caught my eye. It had green handwriting on the back—Aunt Gertrude, age eight. I flipped it over, revealing a black and white newspaper clipping. Two police officers were standing behind a group of children lined up against a brick wall. First two young boys, followed by a girl. Then another boy. And then, my heart sank to my stomach. The prettiest set of light brown eyes was staring back at me in this photo.

The little brown-eyed girl. It's the little girl, one among thousands. My finger roamed across the image and stopped on her. No way. There's no way this could be real.

"Dad, who's Aunt Gertrude?"

"Who?" I stretched out the image in his direction. "Oh her, I think she's your mom's aunt or something." He paid no mind to my question and proceeded to examine an old high school basketball trophy he had just dug out of a box.

My mind raced a mile a minute. I didn't know what to do…and then I quickly picked up the album and shuffled through each picture.

Nope…nothing in this album.

Nope, not that one either.

I flipped page after page, album after album, throwing one after the other to the floor. Dad paused his search, noticing my erratic behavior. "What are you doing?"

I didn't answer. Instead, I continued to search. "Aha."

"Who is this?" My arm stretched once again in his direction. I held up an old picture of a couple sitting on a porch swing this time.

There was a young white woman dressed in a white sundress sprinkled with yellow sunflowers. The image froze her expression as she stared into a young black man's eyes. The man had a gentle smile. He wore blue jean overalls that did little to hide his chubby appearance. His left arm was wrapped tightly around her waist, but it was his right arm that caught my attention. There in his grasp was an old, weathered guitar.

While staring down at the photo, my dad smiled. "That's my great uncle Billy and his wife, Susan. Those two caused a huge stir back in the day." My dad paused and wrinkled his face in my direction, staring. He didn't ask any more questions.

I flipped through three more albums until another picture sent shockwaves through my body. I held up the image. "And this?"

"Uh…don't remember her name, but she's on your mom's side. Some famous singer from back in the day."

I sat back and pressed my back against the cold cement floor. The ceiling was white, nothing remarkable, but I stared at it to find answers. My dad's head popped into frame as he stood over me, looking down.

"Bubble Gum? You alright?"

I smiled. "I will be, Daddie-O. We both will."

And with that, I closed my eyes and welcomed the darkness

THE END

WAIT!!!

Before you go, I would like to take this opportunity to say thank you for reading this book. This was my first book, and I am honored that you took the time to read it. Unless you just flipped through the pages to see if the butler did it. ***Spoiler Alert*** There's no butler in my story. But all kidding aside, thank you again. Please leave a review wherever you purchased the book if you enjoyed the book. Every review helps me improve my writing.

Signed,
Your faithful author,
Rodney LaMarr

For more information on my upcoming projects, please go to my website at: **www.rodneylamarr.com**